the
Mystery
of the
Turtle Lake Monster

the *Mystery* of the *Turtle Lake Monster*

Jeni Mayer

THISTLEDOWN PRESS

Canadian Cataloguing in Publication Data

Mayer, Jeni, 1960-
 The mystery of the Turtle Lake monster

 ISBN 0-920633-68-4

I. Title
PS8576.A93M9 1990   jC813'.54   C90-097074-X
PZ7.M39My 1990

Book design by A.M. Forrie
Cover illustration by Debra Claude
Typeset by Thistledown Press Ltd.

Printed and bound in Canada by
Hignell Printing Ltd., Winnipeg

Thistledown Press Ltd.
668 East Place
Saskatoon, Saskatchewan
S7J 2Z5

Acknowledgements

Jeni Mayer wishes to thank Peter Carver, Nancy Black and Gary Tisdale,
the Penhandlers, "and most especially, my husband Tom."

This book has been published with the assistance of The Canada Council
and the Saskatchewan Arts Board.

To Riki, who believes in rainbows, and Angie, who creates them.

PROLOGUE

It had begun just two short weeks before. Nathan Daniels, well known nature photographer, paddled out on Turtle Lake in his canoe to shoot pictures of loons in their nesting season. But what started out as a normal assignment turned into a mystery involving the Daniels family and many others.

As the sun rose above the water that morning, Nathan brought his canoe close to shore to take a few shots of a pair of loons. Suddenly he heard a loud swishing noise behind him. When he turned, he saw what seemed to be a tree floating across the lake. Moments later the front of the log moved. It was alive. Right before his eyes the log was transformed into a living creature. As it rose higher out of the water, four humps on its back became visible. Nathan's canoe seemed to grow smaller and smaller. The monster was more than twice the length of the small craft and easily twice as wide.

At first the photographer froze with terror. But since the monster seemed to be ignoring him, his fear eased and his curiosity grew. Grabbing his camera, he started snapping shot after shot of the beast. Just when he had exhausted all his film, the monster slowly disappeared into the depths of Turtle Lake.

* * *

Within twenty-four hours everyone around the lake was buzzing with the news. By the next morning the story and Nathan's photographs were splashed across the pages of every newspaper in the country. Within days the resort had gone mad. Every available hotel room was booked; every campsite was filled; and every cabin was occupied.

Scientists from across the country flew in to investigate the monster. Rumour had it that investigators were coming from Scotland to compare the beast to photographs taken of the Loch Ness Monster. The beaches were crowded with sightseers all hoping to catch a glimpse of the monster of Turtle Lake.

CHAPTER ONE

Justin Daniels's whole body trembled with excitement as he peered through his binoculars. His hands shook so much that the image of the four-humped creature bobbed up and down as he looked. Finally he was able to steady himself and focus on the beast's head. At that moment the prehistoric monster changed direction and looked at the beach. Its eyes seemed to be staring right at the dark-haired boy. Justin's heart raced. Then, as suddenly as it had appeared, the creature slid silently into the lake—and was gone.

Justin let the glasses slide to his chest where they hung suspended by a strap around his neck. His mouth felt dry but his palms were sweating. As the excitement overtook him, he began to jump up and down. "I saw it, I saw the Turtle Lake Monster!" he shouted.

But there was no one around to hear him. He was standing on a secluded outcropping of rock that extended out from a stretch of land called Pown Beach. The ledge pushed its way out into the waters of Turtle Lake. It was cut off from the other beaches by a snarl of trees and slippery rocks on both sides. The only way to get to the ledge was through the thick mosquito-infested bush off the main road.

The walk through the trees was long and treacherous. Mosquitoes hung patiently in clouds waiting to attack. But Justin barely noticed them now. He had been bitten so many times in the last two weeks.

The trees grew in peculiar directions. Some grew so tall that you could barely see their tops. Willows grew in tangles along the ground seeking light in the recesses of the cool overcrowded forest. One wrong step and the branches would snap up into the air, often scratching their unsuspecting victim. Justin's arms and legs were covered with small scratches from them.

Justin thought the trip was worth all the trouble once he reached the quiet unpopulated ledge. Unlike the other beaches on the lake, the ledge wasn't crowded with people, each hoping to catch a glimpse of the monster.

Normally Turtle Lake was a quiet resort community, though there was always some confusion during the first week of June. At this time each year, the summer residents moved in and the population grew from 500 winter inhabitants to more than 2500. But this had not been a normal year. In fact, this had been the most unusual year that Turtle Lake had ever seen.

Justin was filled with excitement as he thought over the past week's events. He could hardly believe that he had finally seen the monster with his own two eyes—the same monster that his father, Nathan Daniels, had photographed just two short weeks ago. He thought he would burst with excitement if he didn't tell someone about it soon. One glance at his watch told him that he had better get moving if he was going to make it back to the main road to meet his father at the prearranged time.

Retracing his steps through the bush went more quickly than it had every day for the past two weeks. But that stood to reason, since this was the first time that Justin had actually seen the monster in the flesh. He ran as fast as he could.

He spotted his father's car just as he came out from between two giant black pines. Justin raced forward as the car rolled to a stop. He was breathless by the time he had the car door open.

"Dad, you won't believe it!" he said between gasps. "I saw him, Dad, I really saw him!" His eyes were two huge round circles as he slid onto the seat beside his father.

"You're kidding!" his father said with enthusiasm as he ruffled the dark hair on his twelve-year-old son's head. "You'd better slow down and catch your breath before you pass out."

Justin tried to calm himself. He took deep breaths, then more slowly began to explain. "I saw the monster, Dad... and he was huge and green and scaly... just like the pictures that you took of him." His voice rose with a surge of excitement.

Mr. Daniels listened intently as Justin rushed on.

"...And he stopped and looked right at me, Dad," Justin exclaimed.

His father reached across the seat and playfully patted Justin on the knee as he spoke. "Well, son, I'm glad to hear that I'm not the only one that saw it. I was really starting to think I'd gone off my rocker."

"Well, you haven't," Justin assured him with a huge smile. "But boy, is he ugly," Justin started in again with his animated description. Mr. Daniels looked at his son with keen interest as if he were reliving his own encounter with the beast.

It was several moments before Justin began to slow down. Now that his story was told, a look of contentment settled over his face.

"Well, what are you going to do with your time now that you've finally seen the beast yourself?" Mr. Daniels asked when Justin eventually paused for a breath of air.

"I'm just getting started, Dad!" Justin nearly shouted, with a renewed rush of emotion. "I want to know where the creature lives and how old he is. I want to know everything there is to know about him. And I intend to find out. You just wait and see."

Mr. Daniels rolled his eyes at his son in feigned exasperation.

"Oh, oh, I see trouble coming," he said playfully. "BIG, BIG trouble!"

CHAPTER TWO

Justin could see the large sign looming ahead as his father's car sped closer to their summer home: TURTLE RIVER CAMP-GROUND, LEASE LOTS AND CAMPSITES, NO VACANCY. The words stood out boldly, painted black and outlined in bright, barnyard red.

This was Justin's home away from home in the summer-time. His parents had bought the small resort property several years ago and they had spent the summer there each year. Justin's job was to clean the washrooms and shower house each morning. It wasn't such a bad job if he put his mind to it. He had to mop the floors, clean the toilets, wipe down the sinks, and polish the mirrors. It took him less than an hour. After that, his day was free to do as he pleased.

As the car turned into the campground Justin spotted a black station wagon parked beside his family's trailer. He let out a whoop of delight. His best friend, Kiel Roland, and his family had finally arrived. They had planned on coming a week earlier, but when Mrs. Roland had sprained her ankle their trip had been postponed.

Justin rushed out of the car. He hadn't seen Kiel since the last day of school. They had barely had time to compare their seventh grade report cards before his parents had come to pick him up for their trip to Turtle Lake. As he ran the short distance to his family's trailer, excitement bubbled up inside of him. A huge smile lit his face as he spotted his blond-haired friend lounging in a hammock on the deck. A familiar black cap sat lopsided on Kiel's head. A patch of bright red freckles covered his nose.

"Kiel! Kiel! You won't believe what I saw!" Justin burst out. "I saw the Turtle Lake Monster!"

"Oh, sure you did," Kiel said. "And did you ask him over for supper, too?" Kiel's voice was teasing as usual.

Justin laughed at him. "Actually, I did ask him over. But he said he'd already made plans for the night."

"Well, what do you expect, you dummy? What monster would want to have supper with you?" Kiel said, standing up and taking a playful punch at his friend.

Justin easily side-stepped the blow, then smiled down at Kiel whose head barely reached Justin's chin.

They were both laughing happily when Kiel's ten-year-old sister Katie came out of the trailer and joined them on the deck. The smile disappeared from Justin's face the moment he saw her. Justin couldn't stand Katie.

As Justin scowled at her, he realized that some might think that Katie was quite pretty. She had dark eyes and long black hair that shone in the bright morning sunshine. She was taller than her brother, though she was two years younger. As she came out onto the deck, she stared Justin almost squarely in the face.

Justin stared back at her coldly. Every time she was around him, his hackles rose. He hated the way she was constantly hovering around whenever he and Kiel were together. And what bugged him the most was that Kiel didn't seem to mind. He just treated Katie as though she was one of the boys.

Another thing that drove Justin nuts was Katie's argumentative manner. She seemed to love to argue. If Justin said something was white, Katie would immediately say it was black. And within seconds the fight would be on.

Katie's voice tore Justin out of his thoughts and he stared at her coldly.

"You're such a creep, Jus. There's no such thing as the Turtle Lake Monster and you know it."

"Oh, what would you know about it, Katie?" Justin snarled. "I suppose you don't even read the papers. You've always got your face in some stupid computer screen." A kind of anger grew in his chest as he thought of the time that Katie had beaten him out in the Computer Programming Contest at school. He could still recall the smug look on her face as the principal had awarded her the first prize trophy.

"And I suppose you believe everything you read in the papers," Katie sneered. "Look who's talking about being dumb. HA!" She threw her head back, her dark eyes sparkling with contempt.

Mr. Roland came out onto the deck just then. "Now, now, you two. I hope you're not fighting already," he said sternly. "I wish you'd at least try to get along." He looked hard and long at each of them as he spoke.

The air was charged as Justin and Katie glared contemptuously at each other. Finally Justin pulled his eyes away and looked at Katie's father.

"Okay, Mr. Roland, we'll try not to fight," he conceded. Secretly he was sure he couldn't get along with Katie even if he was tied to a chair with a gag on his mouth.

"Why don't you three go to the beach for a swim?" Mr. Roland suggested with a relieved smile.

"But, Mr. Roland," Justin protested, "can't Katie go by herself?" He gave the older man a beseeching look.

"Justin, you know that Katie doesn't know anyone else at the lake. You take her with you until she makes a few friends of her own," Mr. Roland said firmly.

Justin was about to protest, but he knew it was useless arguing. This was Katie's and Kiel's first trip to Turtle Lake and he supposed that it was his responsibility to see that they had a good time. With reluctance he nodded his head, then disappeared into the trailer to change into his swimming trunks. Katie and Kiel did likewise, and within moments they were headed for the beach.

The resort was buzzing with activity as the three youngsters followed the main road to the beach. An endless stream of cars rolled by, and the shouts of children filled the air.

The boys resumed their talk about the monster as they strolled along.

"Where did you see the monster anyway?" Kiel asked, looking curiously at Justin.

"From my secret hiding spot," Justin replied. "It's the only place at Turtle Lake that isn't crowded with people." He gestured to the endless activity around them. "The Chamber of Commerce has put up a reward for anyone that can prove that the creature truly exists. It's been like this ever since," he said, motioning to the crush of people on the beach.

A television crew was set up on the sand. A crowd of people were jostling for position before the cameras. It appeared, Justin decided, that everyone was anxious to tell their thoughts on the creature.

Kiel's voice drew Justin's attention away from the activity on the beach and he turned to his long-time friend.

"Tell me all about the monster," Kiel begged.

"He's real ugly," Justin replied, anxious to tell his friend all about what he had seen. "He has two huge black eyes that kind of stare right through you."

"Like the devil's eyes?" Kiel asked, caught up in Justin's description.

"Yeah," Justin agreed. "Big beady eyes. And he's huge, with four humps on his back that kind of ripple when he moves."

"Wow!" Kiel said. His own eyes were two round circles.

"And he smells really bad," Justin added for effect. "Like rotten meat."

"Really?" Kiel asked.

"Nah," Justin said, laughing. "He was too far away for me to smell him. But he sure is ugly though."

Kiel shoved Justin playfully. The unexpected attack sent Justin sprawling onto the grass on the edge of the road. Both boys burst into laughter as Kiel put his hand out to help Justin back to his feet only to be dragged down onto the grass as well. Immediately the boys began to wrestle.

"That's the most ridiculous tale I've ever heard," Katie snickered. Her voice was filled with sarcasm.

The boys stopped wrestling, and their laughter died away. Justin stared up at her angrily. He gave her a dirty look in hopes of silencing her, but it only spurred her on.

"If you really believe there is a monster, Justin, why don't you take us to your secret hiding place and let us see for ourselves?" she taunted him. "Unless, of course," she added, throwing her long black hair over her shoulder and placing her hands on her hips, "you're making it all up."

The pose she struck was a blatant challenge, Justin thought. And though he would sooner have spent the day without Katie anywhere around, he could never refuse a dare. Of course, this had gotten him into a great deal of trouble over the years, but he simply couldn't refuse.

"Maybe I'll do just that," he sneered as he got to his feet. He helped Kiel up as well, then crossed his arms across his chest. He stood glaring at Katie with his nose dangerously close to her face.

Katie stared back at him skeptically. "I just bet," she said, her dark eyes flashing. Abruptly, she turned on her heels and marched across the street to the beach.

Justin mumbled angrily under his breath, after making up his mind to take Kiel and Katie to his secret ledge. He only hoped that the monster would go along with his plans and show up to prove her wrong.

He pushed the thought from his mind as he and Kiel burst into a run, easily catching up to Katie. They were all silent as they ran headlong into the water, weaving in and out of the crowd on their way.

They swam out to a free-floating dock, where the water was over their heads. Throughout the afternoon they dove into the cool lake over and over again, each time with a ridiculous dive that had a ridiculous name—like the ten-toe-up-flip-over, and the bottom-up-and-over-tumble-down.

They were all laughing loudly when their parents came to call them in for supper.

That evening both families sat by the fire talking about the monster.

"I don't know what to think about this creature," Mr. Roland said as he handed his wife the pictures that Mr. Daniels had taken of the monster.

"I don't know what to believe any more either," Mrs. Roland said as she gazed at the strange creature in the photographs. "But with all this talk going around I'm certainly beginning to wonder."

"One way or the other, it sure is good for business!" Mr. Daniels said, gesturing to the campground that was overflowing with campers. They all began to laugh.

As Justin lay in bed that night he looked out his bedroom window and saw the brightest star. He made a wish. He wished that he would see the monster again tomorrow when Kiel and Katie were there to see it too.

He grinned as he thought about his wish. He could just picture Katie's face when the creature surfaced. It would be fun to watch her go screaming through the bush calling for her Mommy. He fell asleep with the grin still on his face.

CHAPTER THREE

The next morning dawned bright and warm. Justin awoke to the sounds of loons calling across the lake. Anxious to get his chores done, he jumped out of bed. He quickly washed, brushed his teeth and got dressed. He stopped in the kitchen just long enough to say good morning to his parents, then rushed out the door.

He was running across the campground to the shower house when he heard someone calling him. Turning back towards the trailer, he saw Kiel and Katie coming his way.

"Hey Jus, whatcha doing?" Kiel asked. Once again the black cap was sitting lopsided on his head. He ran the short distance to Justin's side. Katie came up moments later and paused beside her brother.

"I've got to clean the shower house and the bathrooms," Justin explained. He leaned over and straightened Kiel's hat. Kiel laughed, then rearranged his cap so that it once again sat crookedly on his head.

"We'll help," Kiel said, then looked at his sister who nodded silently.

Justin stared at Katie, expecting her to put up a protest at Kiel's suggestion. But her face was impassive.

"Let's do it then," Justin said happily. The offer of help was almost too good to be true.

The job took very little time with the three of them working together. Breakfast was ready by the time they were

finished, and they ate heartily. After breakfast Justin convinced his father to drive them over to Pown Beach. Justin
borrowed his father's binoculars for Kiel to use, then slung
his own over his shoulder. Katie retrieved another pair from
their family car, and within moments they were off to Pown
Beach.

The newcomers' faces fell when they got out of the car
and saw the thick bush they had to walk through. Justin was
almost relieved when they hesitated. He thought for a moment that they were going to refuse to go, but today wasn't
his lucky day. They both took a valiant step towards the
trees.

As they made their way through the thick trees Justin
almost felt sorry for Katie and Kiel. Katie stepped on wild
rose bushes and fell flat on her face trying to run away from
a tree root that looked like a garter snake. Kiel tripped over
a tree stump and got a large mosquito bite on the end of his
nose. The strap on his binoculars got tangled up in the
underbrush, and it took them more than five minutes to
unwind the strap from the tangled mess.

Justin, who was now familiar with the perils of the bush,
negotiated the walk with little trouble. As he glanced back
at Katie and Kiel, who were straggling behind, he couldn't
help remembering his own first few trips to Pown Beach.

By the time they came bursting onto the rock ledge Katie
and Kiel looked as though they had been through a war.
They flopped down on the rocks with loud groans.

Justin had to bite his lip to keep from laughing as he
looked at the two of them resting on the rock. Kiel's nose

was red and swollen, while Katie had smudges of dirt on her cheeks and chin. Her hair was full of dried leaves and grass.

"You came this way every day for two weeks?" Kiel asked Justin incredulously as he distractedly pulled burrs from his socks, then rubbed at his swollen nose.

Justin only nodded. He was trying to keep a straight face.

Both boys turned to look at Katie at the same time. Kiel burst into gales of laughter at the sight she made. Justin could no longer contain his amusement and he fell to the ground in a fit of giggles.

"I don't know what's so darn funny," Katie yelled. "I don't see anything around here that's funny, you jerks!"

"That's because you can't see yourself, Katie," Justin said, laughing. Katie jerked her head back in anger and glared at him. As she turned to her brother though, the angry look disappeared. The sight of his swollen nose sent her into an explosion of giggles.

When their laughter finally subsided, the three sat looking out at the waters of Turtle Lake.

Justin's eyes searched the glassy surface of the lake for any ripple that might hint at the presence of the Turtle Lake Monster. Alternately, he used his binoculars to scan the beach five kilometres away on the other side of the lake.

For hours they stayed there, getting up every few minutes to ease their stiff muscles. After a while they saw a fisherman in a small aluminum boat who waved as he went by. Then they saw a pair of loons that landed on the water a few feet from where they sat. They saw a girl go speeding by on skis behind a high-powered speed boat. They saw everything that one would expect to see at a lake. They did not see the monster.

Justin dropped his binoculars into his lap, then checked his watch and saw that nearly three hours had passed. His spirits fell. He didn't think he could stand the taunting from Katie if the Turtle Lake Monster didn't show up. Only a few minutes were left before they had to start back to meet his father on the main road.

Having spent two weeks on the ledge waiting to see the monster, Justin knew the situation was almost hopeless. As each moment passed he felt more and more depressed. Taking one last look at his watch, he announced that it was time to go back.

One glance at Katie told Justin that he had been right. She had a smirk on her face that meant she was about to make a smart remark.

Justin stiffened, awaiting her outburst. He watched angrily as she put her hands on her hips and glanced at him mockingly. Just then Justin heard a loud splashing noise. It sounded as if a thousand fish had jumped to the lake's surface at once. He spun around, gazing along the surface of the water. Katie and Kiel looked back toward the lake as well. They all froze in shocked silence.

The creature was no more than 200 metres away, directly in front of them, moving slowly across the water. The four humps on its back seemed to move up and down with the waves. Its head rose up out of the water and then sank down again. Katie stood speechless. Kiel stood beside her in shocked silence. Justin watched, unmoving, as the beast

24

slowly made its way across the lake. Its dark green skin looked almost black in the brilliant sunlight.

Suddenly the creature changed direction and turned towards the opposite shore. Now only its back was visible as it moved towards Indian Point.

Indian Point was a large piece of shoreline that projected into and above the lake. Its huge towering cliffs jutted out into the water like a giant fist. This was where the creature seemed to be going.

Justin raised his binoculars to his eyes as the creature moved away. Katie and Kiel followed suit. They all watched silently as the monster slid smoothly across the lake and to the right of Indian Point. It edged closer and closer to the shore. Its body seemed near enough to brush against the branches that clung to the rock face. For several moments, the creature moved along the cliff wall. Then suddenly it was gone. It had disappeared without a trace.

"Where did it go?" Justin muttered to no one in particular. He re-adjusted the focus on his binoculars and scanned the distant shore. He was certain that the creature had not submerged. The water around the cliff was shallow and rocky. It seemed almost impossible to Justin that the creature had simply disappeared.

"It couldn't have just vanished!" Kiel said as he tugged at his cap distractedly. "It just couldn't have."

"It's impossible, but that's exactly what happened. It just disappeared into thin air," Katie said. There was a stunned expression on her face as her binoculars slid down her chest.

Justin remained silent as he tried to figure out how the Turtle Lake Monster could have been there one moment and mysteriously gone the next.

CHAPTER FOUR

The next morning, as Katie, Justin and Kiel were returning from the beach, Mr. Daniels met them outside the trailer with surprising news.

"A reporter just called from the North Battleford *Tribune*. They want to come here and speak with you kids about your monster sighting," he told them.

"I can't believe it," said Katie. "They want to interview *us* about the Turtle Lake Monster?"

"That's right, Katie," Mr. Daniels replied with a smile. "It seems you kids are the first to spot the monster since I photographed it. It would appear people can't keep a secret at Turtle Lake," Mr. Daniels said, laughing.

Justin was thrilled at the prospect of having his name in the paper. It would give him a chance to rub the monster in Katie's face. That would certainly teach her a lesson for being so darn cocky.

"Of course, I told him that you wouldn't be interested in having your pictures in the paper," Mr. Daniels said slyly.

"Oh no!" Justin exclaimed. He couldn't believe his father would do such a stupid thing. "Tell us you really didn't say that," he begged.

Katie and Kiel stood stiffly waiting for his reply.

Mr. Daniels burst out laughing. "I'm only kidding. The reporter will be here in half an hour. So I suggest you get out of those wet bathing suits and into something more presentable." He turned then and left the three behind to discuss the news as he disappeared into the trailer.

The moment the door closed behind him, Kiel began to shout.

"We're going to be famous!" he bellowed gleefully. He was nearly jumping up and down with excitement.

"Yeah, I can see the headline now," Justin joked. "Three nearly naked youths tell tale of monster." He drew a pattern in the air as though the words were written there.

Kiel looked down at his damp swimming trunks and rushed away from the trailer with a yelp.

Katie giggled as she raced after him.

Within minutes everyone was back seated in the living room.

Justin was wearing blue dress pants and a matching sweater that he had brought to the lake to wear to the local Saturday night dances. The outfit was hot and uncomfortable in the morning heat. Kiel looked equally uncomfortable in his fleece-lined jogging suit.

Katie looked cool in a pair of shorts and a T-shirt, her long black hair pulled back into a pony tail.

"Look, there's something I wanted to say before the reporter gets here," Justin whispered. Katie and Kiel leaned forward expectantly. "I don't think we should mention that the monster disappeared at Indian Point."

"Why not?" Katie asked. She looked at Justin quizzically. "Why, that's the best part of the story! It isn't every day that an enormous monster disappears into thin air," she argued.

"Exactly," Justin said. "Can you imagine how many people will rush over to Indian Point if we tell the reporter something like that?" Instantly pictures of overcrowded beaches flooded into his mind. He could easily see thousands of sightseers flocking to Indian Point.

"So what?" Kiel asked with a confused stare.

"So why should we give them a head start?" Justin said with a conspiratorial wink. "Don't forget the $5,000 reward for proof of the creature's existence," he reminded them.

"Are you saying that we should keep it a secret so that we can investigate the Point ourselves?" Kiel asked with growing excitement.

Justin nodded silently. His eyes were twinkling. There was a pause.

"Agreed?" Justin asked, glancing from Kiel to Katie.

"Agreed," Kiel replied immediately.

Justin smiled at his friend, then turned his gaze to Katie. She stared back at him with challenge in her eyes.

"Agreed?" Justin asked, with a hopeful look.

"Oh, I guess so," Katie said reluctantly.

Justin's stomach sank. It was obvious that Katie was bursting to tell the whole world about the creature's strange disappearance.

A loud rap at the door drew away Justin's attention and he raced to answer it. As he opened the door he glanced back at Katie with a pleading stare, then at Kiel with a knowing wink.

He smiled fleetingly as his friend nodded again in silent agreement.

The reporter introduced himself as Sam Lester. He was an older man with steel-gray hair and a round Santa Claus-shaped body. He shook hands with each of them and happily accepted Justin's offer of a cold drink. He took a seat near the window in a tattered rocking chair that looked miles too small for his rotund body.

At first Justin was nervous. He was afraid that Katie might make a slip and let out their secret. But Mr. Lester was so friendly and warm that he soon forgot his worry.

Before long they were all chatting happily. Each told about the monster sighting—except for the part about the monster's disappearance at Indian Point.

Mr. Lester asked each of them about their hobbies, explaining that it helped to fill out the article with bits of personal information.

Katie talked about her love of computers. Kiel told the reporter about his stamp collection. Justin told the reporter how much he liked to read mystery novels and said that he had plans of being a detective when he grew up. He was sure he heard Katie snicker under her breath, but he ignored her.

"You see, Mr. Lester," Justin said seriously, "this is my first real live mystery and I intend to find out all about the monster," he added proudly. "Like how it came to be in Turtle Lake and where it lives."

Mr. Lester looked intrigued at Justin's interest in the beast.

"Do you have any facts to go on?" he asked Justin.

"Oh sure," he replied. "You see, we saw him disap. . ."

Justin stopped suddenly, realizing what he had almost said. He nervously ran his hand through his dark hair. His face turned red with embarrassment as he looked at Katie. He felt ashamed. He had been worried that she wouldn't be able to keep the secret, and here he was blurting it out himself.

His voice came in fits and starts as he tried to cover up his terrible mistake.

" I . . . I . . . I'm sure we'll come up with some clues very soon," he sputtered, then looked down anxiously at his hands.

"I'm sure you will," Mr. Lester said. He did not seem to notice Justin's discomfort. "How about you three posing for a picture?" he asked, setting his notebook on the coffee table beside him.

"Sure!" Justin nearly jumped out of his chair. He was keen to change the subject—anything to distract the reporter from further questions. Justin just wanted the interview to be over.

"Great," Kiel said, as he came to stand beside the distracted Justin.

Within moments, Mr. Lester had the group sitting together on the flowered sofa for the photograph.

Justin tried to look happy, but he didn't feel like smiling. He knew that Katie would give him a terrible time as soon as the reporter was gone. He forced a smile as the flash bulb blinded him momentarily.

The rest of the interview passed in a blur. Justin remained silent as the reporter asked Katie and Kiel a few more questions. Eventually he found himself waving good-bye as Mr. Lester's car pulled away.

"I can't believe I did such a stupid thing," Justin said sheepishly as they watched the reporter's car roll out of sight.

He wanted to be quick to admit his mistake before Katie started in with her smart-aleck remarks.

"Oh, don't worry about it, Jus," Katie said sincerely. "It could have happened to any of us." She smiled at him.

Justin and Kiel looked suspiciously at each other and then at Katie. Justin could hardly believe what he was hearing. It certainly wasn't like Katie to miss the opportunity to razz him about his mistake.

"Well, I'm going to tell Mom and Dad about the interview," Katie said as she rushed out of the trailer.

When she was gone Justin looked at Kiel and shook his head. "Who can understand girls anyway?" he said. He shrugged his shoulders.

"Certainly not me, old buddy," Kiel laughed. He gave Justin a playful punch on the arm.

Justin gave Kiel a shove and sent him stumbling towards the sofa, where he collapsed with a giggle.

As Kiel's laughter faded, Justin glanced out the window and saw Katie flying across the yard towards her parents' tent.

As he watched her retreating form, he couldn't help admitting that maybe Katie wasn't so bad after all. In fact, he thought he might even like her a little bit.

No, he decided, that wasn't possible. Or was it?

CHAPTER FIVE

"Thanks for the ride, Dad," Justin said the next morning as he stepped from his father's big blue Ford onto the road that wound along Golden Sands, a long stretch of beach on the south-east side of Turtle Lake. It was several kilometres down the beach from Indian Point. Katie stepped out behind him.

"Good-bye, Mr. Daniels. See you in a few hours," Kiel called out as he joined them at the edge of the road.

Justin, Katie, and Kiel turned to the large building behind them as the car sped away.

"Wow! Would you look at this place," Kiel said as he motioned with the sweep of his arm to the sparkling new hotel on the waterfront. A large sign out front read: WELCOME TO THE CRYSTAL PALACE HOTEL.

"Yeah, isn't it something," Justin said as he too gazed at the magnificent three-storey structure that was studded with windows. "Two guys from the States built it a couple of years ago," he explained as they walked along the sidewalk that led to the front entrance.

"It must have cost a fortune," Katie commented as she followed Justin and Kiel through a set of double doors that led into the lobby.

"So I've heard," Justin replied. "But it shouldn't take long to pay for it with this crowd."

The lobby was bustling with tourists. Handsomely clad bellhops were racing in every direction pushing carts stacked high with luggage.

"Is it always this busy?" Kiel asked incredulously as they fought to jostle their way through the crowd.

"Not until the monster decided to put in an appearance," Justin replied. He could still remember the vacant lobby that had been commonplace last summer. There had even been rumors that the hotel owners might go broke. But all of that had changed now, Justin thought. The NO VACANCY sign out front was proof of that.

"Are you telling me that all these people are here on the off-chance that they might see the monster?" Kiel said with astonishment.

"Yup!" Justin smiled.

"I thought we were going to rent a boat," Katie said, looking around at the crush, oblivious to the boys' conversation.

"We are," Justin said, pulling his gaze away from the busy activity around him. "The hotel owners rent boats over there." Justin gestured to a set of doors that led off to the right. A small sign overhead read: Boat Rentals.

Justin began propelling himself through the fray with numerous "excuse me's."

The constant noise abated when they stepped into the rental office and the door closed soundlessly behind them. The office overlooked the lake through a series of long floor-to-ceiling windows. The deep blue of the lake gleamed in the bright morning sunshine.

The office itself was decorated in subtle blues. Potted plants were tucked carefully in all the corners. Justin felt as though he was standing in a tropical oasis as he gazed around.

"Well, speak of the devil," a voice boomed out.

Startled, Justin wheeled around, then paused as he saw a skinny red-haired man watching him.

Justin recognized him immediately. It was Mr. Lawford, the owner of the hotel. Justin had seen him on numerous occasions over the past two summers, though they had never spoken.

Justin dragged his eyes away, realizing that he was staring, then let his gaze slip to an older, burly looking man, seated almost out of sight behind him. This must be Herb Schmidt, Mr. Lawford's partner, Justin thought. He looked just as people had described him. His face was set in a permanent scowl and he looked mean and grumpy. He didn't smile at Katie when she said hello. He just mumbled under his breath and turned away.

Justin noticed that in front of the red-haired man a newspaper was spread out, opened to the second page. The headline "THREE YOUNG DETECTIVES VOW TO UNRAVEL THE MYSTERY SURROUNDING TURTLE LAKE MONSTER" stood out boldly.

"Well, well, if it isn't the three famous detectives," Mr. Lawford said, pushing a stray piece of red hair out of his eyes.

"So you figure you're going to discover the mystery of the monster, eh?" Mr. Schmidt said, rising up from his chair.

"We're certainly going to try," Justin said cheerfully, ignoring the man's abrupt manner.

"What can we do for you today, then?" The older man asked in a more business-like tone.

"We'd like to rent a paddle-boat, sir," Justin said, then looked out at the barren strip of fenced-in shore property that usually held the rental boats.

"As you can see," Mr. Lawford said, glancing out the window, "all our boats are out. But if you want to come back in an hour, I'm sure we'll have one for you then."

"Okay, we'll do that," Justin said, trying to keep the edge of disappointment out of his voice. He was anxious to get their investigation of Indian Point underway.

"See you then," the old man said, settling back down in his chair.

Justin turned to Katie and Kiel who were standing quietly nearby.

"Let's wait in the coffee shop," he said, and led them back into the crush of people in the lobby.

"If we can get there," Kiel said as they started through the crowd to the coffee shop on the far side of the building.

The large room was just as busy. Waitresses were bustling about while busboys rushed to clear tables. Summer people in shorts and bathing suits filled almost every seat.

"Over there," Justin said, pointing to a vacant table at the back of the large room.

As they walked down the aisle, Justin could hear many people discussing the Turtle Lake Monster. It was as if everyone's curiosity had been captured by the prehistoric beast.

Justin led the other two to the table, and they all plunked down in the cool metal chairs.

Several people recognized them from the morning paper. Many came to their table to ask them questions about what they had seen. It appeared that the Turtle Lake Monster was one subject that everyone was interested in. Justin sat back and enjoyed all the attention.

Even Katie seemed to be enjoying their new found celebrity status. Her voice was animated as she spoke of the creature they had seen from the outcropping on Pown Beach.

When an hour had passed, the group hurried back to the boat rentals office.

Justin barely noticed the crowd as he edged toward the office. His excitement was growing at the prospect of investigating the monster's disappearance. He could see that Katie and Kiel were equally anxious. They were both racing to keep up.

The red-haired man smiled brightly at Justin as they entered the office.

"You folks are just in time. Your boat just came in," he said.

"Great!" Justin said as he pulled a few crumpled bills from the pocket of his shorts.

"How long will you be wanting the boat for?" the older man asked as he rose from his chair.

"We shouldn't need it for more than an hour or two, sir," Justin replied quietly, as he handed the bills to Mr. Lawford.

"I hope you aren't planning on going over to Indian Point," he said as he straightened out the crumpled dollars. "I hear the water has got pretty rough over there," he added.

"Really?" Justin said curiously.

"Yeah," the older man piped up, "it's been really nasty over there lately."

"Best just to stay as far away as possible from Indian Point," the red-haired man said. He looked at Justin solemnly.

Justin shivered as he considered the warning. Did he have enough boating experience to handle the rough water off the Point? Probably not, he decided. But he instantly shook the doubt from his mind. He was not about to let a little rough water keep him from exploring Indian Point.

He was more determined than ever to get their investigation underway.

CHAPTER SIX

Mr. Lawford opened a large bin moments later as the group stepped outside into the bright sunshine.

"Don't forget to wear these," he said, handing each of them a bright yellow life-jacket.

"You bet," Justin said as he took the life-jacket and hastily strapped it on. He waited anxiously as Katie and Kiel strapped theirs on as well.

Mr. Lawford waved good-bye as Justin, Katie and Kiel ran the short distance along the sand to the lone paddle-boat on shore.

The red-haired man retreated back into the rentals office as Justin and Kiel pushed the boat off the beach and into the water. Justin held the boat steady as Katie and Kiel stepped into it, then heaved himself aboard as well.

"Are you still planning on going to Indian Point?" Katie asked as the boys began to pedal the small craft into deeper water.

"Of course," Justin replied. "Why shouldn't we?"

"But what about the warning?" she asked, glancing back at the boat rental office.

"Oh, don't worry about that," Justin said flippantly. " A little rough water never hurt anyone."

"Yeah, right," Katie mumbled, setting her hands nervously in her lap.

"Hey, Jus," Kiel's voice broke in, "do you know that kid over there?" He pointed to the shore.

Justin turned to look and his eyes came to rest on a boy of about fourteen with black curly hair. He was staring intently at the threesome as they sailed by.

Justin felt shivers shoot up his spine at the penetrating look. It was almost as if the boy was staring right through him.

"No," Justin answered Kiel's earlier question. "I've never seen him before in my life."

"I wonder why he's staring at us?" Katie said in a hushed whisper.

"Beats me," Justin said, trying to shake the odd feeling of coldness that had enveloped him. "Probably just some weirdo," he added, pulling his gaze back to the lake.

As he resumed pedalling, Justin tried to shove the feeling of being watched from his mind, but it would not be denied. He glanced back at the beach anxiously, and his heart skipped a beat. The black-haired boy was still staring sombrely at him.

Justin pedalled with renewed vigour. He was anxious to put distance between himself and the strange boy. Indian Point was still far off in the distance.

Justin was still feeling uneasy as the cliffs of Indian Point became more visible on the horizon.

He shoved the unsettling thoughts from his mind and pedalled faster towards the point.

Indian Point jutted out more than ten metres into the waters of Turtle Lake. The three sides of the point were towering cliffs that burst up out of the lake and hovered more than seven metres into the air.

From a distance Justin could see a sprinkling of cabins sitting peacefully on top of the cliff. But as the boat drew nearer, the cabins disappeared and only the sheer walls of the cliff were visible from the vantage point of their paddle boat.

Justin looked at the cliff with a fresh eye. The walls of the steep bank were sheer rock in some places, and in others wild roses and cacti thrust themselves from white-brown soil. The roots of several large trees on top of the cliff grew like gnarled fingers out through the sides of the cliff. Some of the roots extended all the way down the steep embankment and into the shallow water below. Thick strands of vine-like moss hung loosely overall, almost obliterating the sheer rock walls.

The cliff towered so high overhead that it blocked out most of the bright sunshine. The air around Justin felt cold and goosebumps rose on his arms.

"Boy, would you look at this place," Katie said. She was gazing in amazement at the sheer towering face of the cliff.

As they came to within a few feet of the cliff walls, Justin began searching for clues to the monster's disappearance.

The water below the boat was shallow and transparent. Justin could see rocks of all sizes beneath the surface. He was almost certain that the large creature could not have submerged in the shallows.

As they rounded the corner of the cliff Justin immediately noticed that the water was just as shallow. Rocks of various sizes sparkled beneath the lake's surface. He studied them intently as he steered the boat in a complete circle, then moved back the way they had come. Moments later, he stopped pedalling and sat staring blankly at the other side of the lake.

"This is the exact spot where the creature disappeared," he told his friends. "There's our look-out," he said, pointing towards the outcropping of rock on the opposite shore of the lake, that looked miniature in the distance.

"I think you're right," Katie agreed, squinting at the opposite shore.

"This may be the spot, but where could he have gone to?" Kiel said soberly. "The water's no more than three metres deep. There is just no way that he could have submerged here." He stared in bewilderment at the rocky lake bottom beneath the clear water.

"It just doesn't make any sense at all," Justin said with a sinking heart.

"Maybe we imagined the whole thing," Katie said, hopelessly.

"Maybe we did," Justin said. But his voice sounded anything but convinced.

As Justin sat gazing at the shallow water, he replayed the scene from yesterday in his mind. He could remember seeing the creature edging closer and closer to the walls of the cliff. Its head, he remembered, had been well above water when it had suddenly disappeared.

He replayed the scene repeatedly, but could not sort out the strange mystery. There was simply no way that the creature could have submerged in the waters that surrounded Indian Point.

"Well, let's go back," Justin finally said. He was developing a headache and he felt chilled to the bone.

Kiel and Justin pedalled rapidly as they steered the boat back toward the middle of the lake.

Justin was silent as he searched his mind for an answer to the puzzle. The boat glided smoothly into the deeper water in the middle of the lake.

He was so caught up in his own thoughts that it was several moments before he noticed the black clouds building overhead and felt a strong wind blowing in his face.

"There's a storm coming and it looks like a bad one," he said. He extended his arm to point at a huge black cloud moving quickly towards them. "We'd better hurry up."

Kiel followed his lead and began pedalling faster in the direction of the boat rentals office.

It was obvious to Justin that the storm was moving in at a ferocious pace. The wind was gathering speed. It felt harsh and cold against his face.

"Oh no!" Justin shouted moments later as he looked down at the pedals below his feet. Just then, Kiel cried out as well. The pedals on both sides of the boat were spinning madly, but the paddle-wheels that propelled the boat were no longer moving. Somehow the cable connecting the pedals and the paddles must have become disconnected, Justin realized.

He looked around in a panic for oars. But there were none. He held his breath as panic overtook him. Their predicament was worsening by the moment, he realized. The boat was crippled. A terrible storm was upon them and the wind was blowing the boat north into the uninhabited areas of Turtle Lake.

Justin knew that if the wind continued to push them northward there would be no one around to save them. The north end of the lake was nothing but barren beaches and untamed forest.

"Paddle with your hands," he shouted.

Kiel and Katie jumped into action, plunging their arms into the cool water of the lake, struggling to propel the boat forward.

"It's useless," Kiel's voice was a wounded cry moments later. "Whenever we start to move forward, the wind and the waves push us back even farther."

"Don't give up," Justin encouraged him. But he could see that his friend was right. They were going nowhere fast. The hotel owners had been right after all.

Justin's heart sank. He knew they were headed for grave danger. They were helpless as the storm raged around them.

CHAPTER SEVEN

"Help! Help!" Katie shouted.

Justin's head spun around at her sudden outburst. He wondered fleetingly who Katie was calling to, then he too caught sight of two people on the beach, off to the right. He began to wave frantically to the couple in the distance.

"Heeeeeelp!" Katie shouted again, but the strangers on the beach simply waved back, as if unable to understand her repeated calls above the thunder that roared overhead. They turned and ran to a large white cabin as the rain began pelting down.

The last of the cabins passed by in a blur as the boat gained speed. It reminded Justin of a ride he had been on at the fair. It was terrifying rushing along out of control. But unlike the fair ride it seemed as if the boat would never stop.

Justin looked at the frightened faces of Katie and Kiel beside him. He immediately felt guilty for getting them into this awful situation. He knew that he should have heeded the warning of the hotel owners.

"It'll be all right," he said, trying to sound optimistic. "When we don't show up to meet Dad, he'll come looking for us." He tried to soothe them, but they could hardly hear him over the roar of the rising storm. Though he said nothing more out loud, Justin only hoped that his father would find them in time to save them from disaster.

Water began splashing over the sides of the boat as the waves grew higher and wilder. Rain poured down in torrents, adding to the water that was quickly filling up the boat.

Working together as a team, Justin, Katie and Kiel began bailing with cupped hands. But for every handful that they threw overboard, twice as much came splashing back in with the waves and the rain. The boat seemed to be filling up with alarming speed.

Katie was the first to spot the island appearing on the horizon.

"Look!" she yelled excitedly, pointing to a small uninhabited chunk of land that loomed larger and larger through the sheets of rain.

"It's Spruce Island," Justin shouted joyfully. He looked at Kiel with a broad smile on his face. But the smile disappeared as Kiel gestured to the water that was flooding the bottom of the boat.

Justin and Katie looked mournfully down at the water rising around their feet.

"We're sinking!" Katie cried. A look of horror spread across her face.

The situation seemed hopeless to Justin. The boat was sinking with each passing second. The island was still more than fifteen metres away and the storm around them was raging fiercely.

The boat moved sluggishly towards the island under its new weight. Suddenly a huge wave pushed up from beneath the bottom of the boat. The small craft hung in mid-air for seconds, on the verge of turning end over end.

Justin reached out frenziedly and gripped the side of the boat as a second wave came crashing from behind. It sent the craft spiralling frantically forward towards the shore of Spruce Island.

The paddle-boat levelled out, and as it did, water rose rapidly, engulfing the seats. The sides of the boat quickly disappeared as the waves overtook them.

"Jump! Jump!" Justin shouted wildly.

Using the sinking boat as a diving board he stood up and took a gigantic leap towards the shore.

Katie and Kiel followed, both leaping from the boat just seconds behind him.

Justin hit the shore with a painful crack, as his elbow made contact with a large rock. Katie landed on her knees with a loud plop.

Kiel, who had misjudged the distance, fell a metre short of the shore and landed with a loud splash in the cool water.

Justin and Katie sprang to their feet, and dragged him out of the water by an arm and a leg.

The small group huddled together. Their clothing was soaked through to their skin. The wind felt like slivers of ice as it tore at Justin's wet body. Silently he watched as the last corner of the orange boat sank in the deep water just two metres from shore.

"What . . . are we . . . going . . . to do?" Katie asked. Her teeth were chattering and her words came out in erratic spurts.

"I don't know," Justin admitted. "It could be days before we're found!"

He scanned the horizon as a fierce wind tore at his clothes. He began to shake, his body vibrating like a jack hammer. He knew that they were at the mercy of the storm on the barren island.

CHAPTER EIGHT

The sky overhead was beginning to darken as the sun dipped in the western sky. Night was rapidly approaching. Justin's watch told him more than eight hours had passed since their paddle-boat had taken its plunge beneath the stormy surface of the lake.

Justin was sitting in the shelter of a clump of ragged weeds with Katie and Kiel huddled close beside him. Their clothes were still soaked and clung to their skin in a damp mass.

"What's that?" Kiel asked as a low rumbling sound filled the air. He stood up, appearing to try to distinguish the sound.

"It's probably just thunder," Katie muttered, not bothering to rise.

"I don't think so," Justin said as he stood up beside his friend. He squinted through the near darkness at the calm water and now cloudless sky. The storm had subsided a while ago. He listened carefully to the rumbling sound as it changed into a loud purring and then into the more distinct buzzing of an outboard motor.

"It's a boat!" he shouted. Excitement rose in his chest.

Katie jumped to her feet and started scanning the lake.

It seemed ages before Justin spotted the blue flag of an R.C.M.P. speedboat.

"We've got to get their attention," Justin said to his friends. He knew that another boat might not come along for hours, if not days. He quickly began shouting and waving his arms in the air.

"Oh no," Katie's voice was a mournful cry as the boat veered away from the island and started toward the distant western shore of Turtle Lake.

Justin thought that Katie looked as though she was about to give up all hope. Her shoulders were slouched in defeat.

Then he nearly jumped out of his skin when she unexpectedly opened her mouth and let out a blood-curdling shriek. He felt shivers going up and down his spine at the piercing sound.

Justin turned his head to see if the scream had its desired effect. Relief flooded him as the driver of the boat turned to look back at the island.

Justin resumed waving fiercely, but it wasn't necessary. The boat was already headed in their direction.

In his excitement, Justin scooped Katie into a huge hug, swinging her feet off the ground with a gleeful shout. Katie's shouts rang in his ears. She smiled at him, then seemed to notice for the first time his arms enfolding her. The colour rose to her cheeks. Justin, realizing what he had done, released her from his embrace, suddenly awkward with embarrassment. He could feel the surge of hot blood to his cheeks and he looked away.

"See, I told you everything would be all right," Kiel said, oblivious to Justin's discomfort.

"Yeah, right," Justin said happily as he forced his embarrassment to abate. He could still recall Kiel's frightened face as they sat on the island's shore. Kiel had been strangely silent for most of the passing hours.

As the boat approached, Justin saw his father sitting in the back. He looked more worried than Justin had ever seen before. Mr. Roland sat beside him looking equally upset.

When the boat finally pulled onto the shore there was a mad rush of kisses and hugs and questions flying in every direction.

"Are you all right?"

"Is anyone hurt?"

"How did you find us?"

"Where's your boat?"

The scene was chaotic, with everyone talking at once. Finally, the policeman restored order by helping the group into the boat and bundling them up in warm woollen blankets. Each of the children was given a cup of steaming black coffee as they sped across the lake.

Though Justin had never drunk coffee before, it tasted incredibly good, the steaming liquid warming his freezing limbs. For the first time in hours he began to feel human.

Kiel took one swallow of the black brew, then wrinkled his nose in disgust. Justin couldn't help chuckling at the expression on his friend's face.

Katie held the cup against her face, as if to warm her reddened cheeks.

"Boy, am I ever glad that you showed up," Katie said to her father through chattering teeth.

"Me too," Justin chimed in. "I was terrified." He shivered more from the thought of what could have happened than from the cold.

"How did you find us anyway?" Kiel asked as he drew his blanket tightly around his shoulders.

"We had a call from a couple who saw you waving at them," the police officer's voice boomed over the roar of the boat's engine. "They thought you might be in danger, what with the storm and all."

"I'd already reported you missing by then," Mr. Daniels broke in.

The sound of Officer Olsen's booming voice radioing ahead for an ambulance cut off any further discussion of their rescue.

"But we're not hurt," Justin protested. All he really wanted to do was to climb into his bed in the trailer and go to sleep.

"Yeah, we're just fine," Katie asserted.

"Don't bother arguing," Mr. Roland piped up. He still had a worried frown pulling at the corners of his mouth. "You could have caught pneumonia out here."

"But Dad . . . " Kiel objected.

"Enough!" Mr. Roland gave his son a firm look.

Justin knew that that was the end of the conversation. "I really don't care where I go," he finally agreed, "as long as it's warm and dry." He laughed.

Kiel nodded in hearty agreement, while Katie's face stared blankly across the water.

The ambulance was waiting for the children when the boat came to shore, and they quickly climbed in.

Justin fell asleep almost as soon as the ambulance got underway. When he finally awoke, as the ambulance was pulling to a stop in front of the hospital, he tried to recall what he was dreaming about. But he could not remember the scene that had been playing in his head. He only had a sense of great uneasiness that lingered like a bad smell.

He tried to force the odd feeling from his mind as the doctor did a thorough examination of him, but he could not. The strange feeling of doom hovered over him like a pall.

His heart sank when the decision was announced that the trio would stay overnight. Justin could tell there was no defying the unyielding Dr. Spencer.

The doctor's voice seemed miles away as he explained his thinking to Mr. Roland and his father. Justin sat silently, only half listening to the lilting Irish voice.

"I think it's wise to keep them in overnight. I'm sure there's nothing to worry about. But there is always the chance of pneumonia."

"I agree totally," Mr. Daniels's voice was also determined.

Justin turned to glance at his father who was nodding his head in agreement. His father gave him a worried frown, then turned back to talk to the doctor. Justin blocked out the conversation. His mind was still searching for clues to his new unexplained feeling of anxiety.

The next few hours went by in a blur. Justin had vague recollections of changing into a pair of garish striped pyjamas and having his temperature taken, but the rest was foggy. The moment he lay down on the warm hospital bed, he was fast asleep.

"It's about time you woke up."

Justin struggled to dispel the fog of sleep as he awoke to the sound of Kiel's teasing words. He pulled himself up to a sitting position just as a pillow came sailing towards him.

Justin caught the pillow full on the face. He grabbed it and prepared to heave it back, then collapsed back on the bed in a fit of giggles. Kiel was propped up on the next bed in a pair of garish pink pyjamas. His black cap, looking the worse for wear after last night's storm, was propped crookedly on his head. The bright morning sunlight that filtered through the hospital windows turned Kiel's freckles into bright red dots.

"You look like an idiot," Justin said between giggles.

"Look who's talking," Kiel said, bursting into laughter.

"Huh?" Justin asked, then glanced down at his own attire. He was wearing a matching set of pink pyjamas. Colour rose to his cheeks as he hurled the pillow at Kiel.

"Well, you two look like you're in good spirits." Justin turned to the familiar voice of the doctor.

Mr. Roland and Mr. Daniels were right behind him, as well as Katie, who was dressed in a fresh pair of jeans and a T-shirt.

"We sure are," Justin said. He was now anxious to get out of the confines of the hospital.

The moment the doctor gave his approval for them to go home, Justin and Kiel rushed out of bed. Their fathers had brought them a set of clean dry clothes and they changed in record time.

An hour later Justin walked into his family's trailer where the smell of freshly made cinnamon buns greeted him. He was suddenly starving, and he invited Katie and Kiel to join him for a snack.

Their mothers hovered over them with worried frowns as they ate.

"Mom," Justin said with growing annoyance, "I feel fine."

"I'm sure you do," Mrs. Daniels said, placing another steaming roll in front of him. "And just think how much better you'll feel after you've spent the day lazing around the house."

"But Mom," Justin protested. "I've got a lot of things I want to do today." He stared at his mother beseechingly.

"Like what?" she asked.

"Well..." Justin mumbled. He couldn't tell his mother that he wanted to resume his investigation of the Turtle Lake Monster.

"Nothing that can't wait till tomorrow," she said in response to his silence. Without giving Justin a chance to argue, she turned on her heels and retreated to the kitchen.

"Great!" Justin muttered. He ran his hands through his hair in aggravation.

Katie and Kiel looked at their own mother who was hovering nearby.

"That goes for you two as well," Mrs. Roland said at their imploring stare. She too turned and walked out of the living room.

The three muttered under their breath until Justin retrieved his Monopoly board, and within minutes the game was underway. The afternoon sped by as the game continued. It was not until Katie owned every hotel in the game and Justin and Kiel were flat broke that the boys finally admitted defeat.

Mr. Daniels came into the trailer just as the children were putting the Monopoly game away. Justin looked up and saw that he had a large envelope in his hands.

"Someone left a letter for you out on the step," Mr. Daniels said, handing the envelope to Justin.

Justin took the letter and ripped it open excitedly. He felt the blood rushing from his face as he read the words inside.

The letter was a series of words that had been cut from a magazine. In a jumble of colours it read: FORGET ABOUT THE MONSTER OR YOU'LL BE IN MORE TROUBLE THAN YOU WERE YESTERDAY. Justin's name was printed on the envelope in small squiggly letters that looked as if it were written by a young child.

Whoever wrote the note knew about the boating accident the day before. Justin realized that news travelled fast in the community, but this was ridiculous. He was also certain that whoever wrote the note meant business.

He felt a chill run down his spine. As he read the note one final time, he felt more fear than he had when he had been stranded on Spruce Island in the storm.

CHAPTER NINE

"I'm sure it's just a prank," Officer Olsen said, carefully picking up the letter by the corner. "But I'll take it back to the station and we'll investigate further, just to make sure." He carefully placed the letter in his briefcase.

Justin sat next to Kiel on the sofa. Both were looking expectantly at the officer who had arrived shortly after Justin had opened the threatening letter.

Justin recalled how he had been afraid to show the note to anyone. He hadn't wanted to worry his parents. But he had soon realized that his parents should know about it, just in case the letter was some kind of sick joke.

"Now back to what I really came to talk to you about." Justin drew his mind out of his thoughts and once again looked expectantly at Officer Olsen. He couldn't help thinking that the policeman was trying to avoid saying whatever it was that he had come to say. The policeman was twisting the rim of his hat in his hands almost nervously.

Finally the officer began to speak.

"We had the paddle-boat brought up from the bottom of the lake and had a mechanic look at it." He shuffled his feet before he continued.

Justin sat forward in his chair, not wanting to miss a word of what the officer was saying.

"It appears that the line that connects the pedalling mechanism to the paddle-wheels had been cut."

Justin heard his mother's sharp intake of breath. He glanced at his father who had turned strangely pale.

"Are you saying that the boat was . . . sabotaged?" Justin asked. The whole idea of it seemed unbelievable.

"So it appears," Officer Olsen said unhappily.

"But who would do such a thing?" Katie asked.

"Actually, I was hoping that you would have a few ideas." The policeman glanced at the three young faces before him.

"I can't imagine," Kiel said hoarsely. "We've only been here a few days. We don't know anyone at the lake." He spoke as if thinking aloud. Katie nodded in silent agreement.

Justin's mind raced. He couldn't imagine why anyone would do such a thing. He gazed around at his parents and the blank faces of Katie and Kiel. Finally his eyes came to rest on the officer's briefcase, and a thought came to mind. Did the author of the poison pen letter have anything to do with the damaged boat, he wondered.

"Well, maybe it wasn't meant for you after all," the policeman said, when no one could come up with a firm idea. "It's possible that you were just the victims of a practical joke." His voice was not at all convincing.

"Some joke!" Justin seethed. He could still recall the fear he had felt when the boat had been rushing along out of control.

"What do you propose we do about this?" Mr. Daniels said. He looked at Officer Olsen with a worried frown.

"There's really not a lot that you can do, I'm afraid," the policeman's wan smile was apologetic. "At least not until we find out who's behind this."

With that, the policeman placed his hat back on his head, retrieved his briefcase, and started toward the door. He had the door halfway open when he turned and glanced at Justin.

"I really don't think there's much to worry about," he said reassuringly, then added. "But it wouldn't be such a bad idea to be cautious for the next few days."

The officer's words were still ringing in Justin's ears moments after he had gone.

"I think you had better forget about any further investigation of the Turtle Lake Monster." Mr. Daniels's voice startled Justin and he snapped his head toward his father. His Dad's face was a worried mask.

"You bet we will," Justin said, looking nervously down at his shoes, then back at his father. It was obvious that his father had caught Justin's expression. Justin was lying and his father wasn't fooled. Deep lines of anxiety around his eyes betrayed his father's worry.

Justin had no intention of letting the mystery alone. If their investigation of the Turtle Lake Monster had something to do with their strange accident, then he had every intention of finding out what it was. He wasn't about to back down now. If anything, he was more anxious than he had been before to get to the bottom of the secret.

But despite Justin's bravado, a sense of foreboding hovered over him. He wondered about the danger that lurked ahead.

CHAPTER TEN

Justin felt terrible the next morning after sleeping only a few hours. It seemed that every time he fell asleep, he was awakened by a horrible nightmare about battered boats and black-eyed monsters.

He was trying not to show how tired he felt. He knew that if his mother noticed, she would insist he was coming down with something. He didn't think he could spend even one more day inside when the sun was shining so brightly outdoors.

He was still feeling sluggish after he had finished cleaning the shower house. He was disappointed that Katie and Kiel hadn't come to help. But after all that had happened he hadn't wanted to wake them so early.

The activity around the campground that morning was almost deafening when he stepped outside and returned his mop and pail to the tool shed. Children were racing around the circular lane on bikes. Their shrieks of laughter filled the air.

As he walked slowly back to his own trailer he heard many campers discussing plans to go looking for the monster in the lake. It seemed as though everyone was searching for the elusive beast.

Thankfully, he thought, no one else was being subjected to sabotaged boats and strange threatening letters.

He could see the happy look of adventure on the campers' faces as they set out on their quest. He wished that his own investigation could be so light-hearted. But he knew that it could not be. There were simply too many strange things happening: too many odd events that seemed to centre around their investigation of the creature.

Justin saw his father waving to him and he rushed to the trailer.

"Morning, Dad," Justin said. He tried to keep his voice cheerful despite the worries he was dealing with.

"Morning, Jus," his father replied. "What are you planning to do today?" His question, though spoken lightly, was packed with dynamite.

Justin knew that his father understood that he wouldn't be able to give up the investigation. In that, they were both very much alike. Neither of them was known for being a quitter.

"Oh, I don't know," Justin replied. "Maybe we'll just hang around the beach."

Mr. Daniels's brows were knit as he gazed at his son. "Well, whatever you decide to do, I want you to be careful." He looked at Justin knowingly.

"I will, Dad," Justin assured him, then gave his father a light smile.

Mr. Daniels smiled back wanly, then informed Justin of his own plans for the day. "Mr. Roland and I are going over to an auction in Glaslyn. Your Mom and Mrs. Roland just left to get a few groceries, but they'll be back in an hour or so."

"Okay," Justin said. "We'll see you later." Justin waved good-bye to his father and Mr. Roland as they sped off in the car moments later. His father's terse last words still rang in his ears.

"Stay out of trouble. And be careful!"

Justin ran to the Rolands' tent as if wild dogs were nipping at his heels. He was anxious to talk to Katie and Kiel about their plans for the day.

Katie and Kiel were slow to get moving that morning. After a great deal of debate, they decided to eat breakfast in the cafe. No one wanted to cook in the rising summer heat. They retrieved their bikes and started for the cafe a short distance away.

Justin, Kiel and Katie had to jostle their way past a group of boys who were sitting on the front steps of the cafe when they arrived a few minutes later. The air conditioning in the restaurant was pumping out at full blast when they entered, and yet the air was hot and humid. They took the first available booth and plopped down tiredly.

"Well, what should we do today?" Justin broached the subject as soon as they had drinks in front of them.

"Let's go to Indian Point again," Katie replied instantly.

"Are you crazy?" Kiel retorted. "Didn't last time scare you enough?" He was staring at his sister as if she had suddenly grown horns.

"Actually, that's what I thought we should do today too," Justin said, giving his friend an apologetic smile. It wasn't often that he and Katie took sides against Kiel.

"You're both nuts," Kiel muttered, arranging his cap with an exaggerated flourish.

"That may be true," Justin retaliated with a short laugh, "but since that's where all the clues lead in our investigation, I can't think of a better place to start."

"I don't know," Kiel muttered, the frown deeply embedded on his face.

"Look, Kiel," Justin said, trying to convince his best friend of his reasoning, "I know we are going to find something important at Indian Point. I can feel it right here." He pressed his hand against his chest dramatically. "There have to be some clues about the monster at the Point." His words ended in a near shout.

Several customers in the restaurant turned their heads in his direction. Justin noticed that he was drawing attention to himself and he instantly closed his mouth.

Tension hung in the air as Justin stared at Kiel. In all the years that they had been friends, they had rarely had an argument. Relief flooded Justin as Kiel finally nodded his head in agreement, even though he did not look totally convinced that going to Indian Point was such a good idea.

"There is one thing I think we should do before we go though," Katie said casually. She flipped her long black hair over her shoulder with the flick of her wrist.

"What's that?" Justin asked.

"I think we ought to check the weather forecast."

Kiel was the first to start laughing. Suddenly the idea of being caught in a second unexpected storm seemed terribly funny and highly unlikely. Justin finally burst into a stream of giggles and Katie rapidly joined in.

"Check the weather forecast," Justin repeated between guffaws. "That's a good one."

A comfortable silence settled over Justin as his laughter subsided. He could hardly believe that he and Katie were actually getting along. He supposed that their mutual interest in the creature was partly responsible for this unusual event. And strangely enough, he thought, it didn't feel so bad being on the same side of the fence for once.

Justin's thoughts were suddenly cut off as a strange coldness enveloped him. He shuddered involuntarily.

"What is it?" Kiel asked, looking questioningly at Justin, who suddenly looked nervous.

"Don't you get the feeling that we're being watched?" Justin asked, as he scanned the faces in the crowded restaurant.

"Not really," Kiel said flatly, but he too began to study the people around them.

"Over there," Justin said, motioning with a toss of his head. They all turned to look at a black-haired boy who was sitting a few metres away in the booth next to theirs. The boy's face was obscured by a magazine that he was reading.

There was something familiar about the cap of black curls, Justin thought, but couldn't put his finger on exactly what it was.

As if sensing that he was being watched, the boy suddenly looked at Justin and blushed guiltily. A flicker of recognition flitted across Justin's memory. It was the boy who had been staring at them on the day of their boating accident.

The boy instantly turned away from Justin's gaze and shifted uncomfortably in his seat. Justin took the opportunity to study him more closely. He was dressed much the same as the other children in the restaurant, in bright-coloured shorts and a T-shirt. But strangely, the boy was also wearing a jean jacket that was covered with shiny silver studs. Justin was sweating in a T-shirt and shorts, and he couldn't imagine how the boy could stand the heat in the jacket.

As the boy tried to bury his face again in his magazine, Justin noticed a small tattoo on his wrist. The word "Blackie" stood out in bright red block letters.

"That's the kid from the beach the other day," Justin whispered, as he looked at Katie and Kiel.

"I wonder what he's doing here," Kiel said curiously.

"Spying on us again," Katie replied confidently, then shivered involuntarily.

"But why?" Justin spoke his thoughts out loud, then wondered briefly if the boy had heard them discussing their investigation of Indian Point. It seemed possible that he had.

Once again the black-haired boy turned to look at Justin. Then he dropped his magazine to the floor and sprang from his seat. As he rushed past their table, he paused. He hovered nearby as if he was about to speak, then seemed to think better of it. He gave Justin a cold glare and rushed down the long aisle.

"Hey, Blackie," Justin called out, remembering the name that had been tattooed on the boy's wrist. But the dark-haired boy ignored Justin's call and rushed out of the building.

"I wonder what that was all about," Justin said when Blackie had disappeared from sight. He couldn't help thinking that the strange boy had seemed almost angry with him. But that didn't make any sense at all. He was certain that he had never seen him before the day of their boating accident. There was no way that he could have forgotten those piercing eyes.

"Who knows?" Kiel said, nervously.

"This whole thing's getting too weird for me," Katie murmured. She was twisting a napkin apprehensively in her hands.

"Me too," Justin muttered under his breath. The strange boy's unexplained animosity was unnerving.

Justin was deep in thought when the waitress finally brought their breakfast. The group's earlier cheery camaraderie had evaporated and they ate in silence.

As soon as they finished eating, they quickly got to their feet and paid for their meals.

Justin was anxious to go to Indian Point and resume their search. He was certain that there must be some clues at the Point that would lead them to the creature.

As they stepped outside, he tried to bring back some of their earlier lightheartedness as they got on their bikes for the short trip home. He told a string of jokes. Most of them drew only groans or mild giggles, but it served to lighten their mood.

The sun was unbearably bright, and the air felt almost suffocatingly hot. Justin turned to Kiel, who was riding slowly beside him, to see if he was being affected by the heat.

"Hot enough for you?" he asked.

"You bet," Kiel said, taking one hand off the handlebars to wipe a trickle of sweat from his brow.

Justin's bike rattled as they rode onto the bridge that spanned Turtle Creek.

Justin turned back to say something to Kiel, then his mouth clamped shut in horror. He watched helplessly as the front wheel of his friend's bike began to wobble erratically. He could see that Kiel was trying desperately to retain control as the bike hurtled forward. Justin's breath caught in his throat as the wheel finally twisted, then came off completely. The back end of the bike suddenly lurched into the air.

Katie's scream pierced Justin's consciousness as the bike flipped into the air, end over end, sending the unsuspecting Kiel high into the air like a rag doll. He landed with a painful crack on the guardrail of the wooden bridge.

"Oh my God!" Justin said, dropping his bike on the road and rushing to Kiel's aid. As he ran he could hear Katie crying out behind him and then in a split second she was at his side.

Justin bolted toward Kiel as he teetered on the guardrail on the verge of plunging headlong into the rocky creek below.

He grabbed Kiel by the leg and grunted as he pulled him back to safety. Katie came up beside him and helped lower Kiel to the ground.

Justin held his breath as Kiel lay perfectly still on the gravel. Crouching there, he recalled all the times that he and Kiel had played war over the years. He had seen Kiel play dead many times, but now real terror gripped Justin. Kiel's body was limp and still. Finally Kiel opened his eyes with a painful jerk.

"Are you okay?" Katie asked, her voice full of concern for her brother.

"I think so," Kiel answered. "Except for my finger," he added, bringing his hand in front of his face.

"I think it's broken," Justin choked. His stomach rolled at the sight of the twisted finger.

"I think you're right," Kiel groaned, then added, "By the way, did either of you get the number of the car that hit me?"

Justin gave a nervous giggle. "No, it was going too fast."

Kiel let out a strangled laugh that quickly faded, and Justin could see that his friend was in a great deal of pain.

"We'd better get you to the campground," he said. "Our mothers should be back from grocery shopping by now."

Carefully Justin and Katie pulled Kiel gently to his feet. He teetered for a moment in obvious agony, as his battered body adjusted to being upright. He seemed to weave erratically, as though hit by a wave of dizziness, then straightened up and stood more steadily.

Justin bent and retrieved Kiel's bike that was lying in the middle of the road. He studied it carefully, wondering what had caused the strange accident. The wheel had completely dislodged itself from the frame. The bolt that held it in place lay on the other side of the road.

Justin walked over, knelt down and picked up the bolt. As he turned it over in his fingers, he couldn't help noticing that it had been sheared in half. But strangely, the bolt did not appear to be cleanly severed, as it should have been if it were merely worn away. Instead it looked as though it had been struck with something. There were jagged gouges in the shiny metal.

A spooky feeling came over Justin as he studied the stretch of road where the accident had happened. He scanned the gravelled surface for any object that might have been large enough to cause this sort of damage, but there was nothing. The damaged bolt was a complete mystery. He shoved the uneasiness out of his mind wordlessly and turned to assist Kiel on the walk back to the campground.

"Can you see what went wrong with the bike?" Kiel asked, noticing Justin's preoccupied look.

Justin shoved the damaged bolt into his pocket distractedly, then looked at Kiel with a feigned smile. There seemed little use in alarming him about his own anxieties. "No, it looks like the bolt snapped in half. It should be easy enough to fix though," he said as he picked up the undamaged wheel that lay on the ground. "Let's get going."

The trip home went slowly, with Justin pushing his own bike and dragging Kiel's behind. Katie walked slowly alongside, as she pushed her own bike with one arm and supported a still wobbly Kiel with the other.

Once back at the trailer, the children were quickly hustled into Mrs. Daniels's small car for the trip to the Turtleford hospital. Kiel gritted his teeth as the car sped along the bumpy road.

The waiting room was empty when they arrived and a nurse swiftly took Kiel in to see the doctor. Everyone sat with worried looks on their faces as Doctor Spencer examined Kiel. Finally, the doctor came out of the examining room with his arm around a stiff and sore-looking Kiel.

"Well, the finger is broken," he told the group, indicating the large bandage on his patient's hand. "But it was a good clean break and should heal nicely," he assured Kiel's mother. "Other than a few nasty bruises and a slightly battered ego, I think your son will be just fine," he said, patting his patient gently on the back.

"Thank you for all your help, Doctor," Mrs. Roland said with a grateful smile on her face. She stood up and put her arm around Kiel, who still looked pale and shaky.

"I hope I won't be seeing any of you again for a while. Two accidents in one week is quite enough, I should think," the doctor said. It was obvious that he remembered them from the boating accident. "You've certainly had a string of bad luck lately," he remarked with a twinkle.

But Justin wondered if luck had anything to do with it. One thing was certain, he thought. Something very strange was going on!

CHAPTER ELEVEN

Justin went over the strange accident in his mind as their family car sped back to the campground. But there seemed to be no easy solution. It was almost as though a black cloud was hanging over their heads.

Justin's heart went out to Kiel, who sat beside him. It was obvious that he was in a great deal of discomfort. His face was a pale mask of pain.

It took Justin a long time to fall asleep that night. All the bizarre events of the past days haunted him: the strange message, the sabotaged boat, the odd angry boy in the cafe and finally Kiel's incredible accident.

When sleep finally overtook him, he was plagued by frightening dreams. He awoke several times during the night, bathed in sweat as gory images raced through his mind.

The next morning Kiel and Katie were still asleep when Justin crossed the campground to do his morning chores. It wasn't until he was finished and on his way back to the trailer that Kiel came hobbling out of the tent, with his sister close behind him.

"How about some scuba diving today?" Justin asked his friend jokingly. "Or maybe some water skiing."

"Oh Lord," Kiel grimaced, "it hurts to even think about it."

"Well then, how about some breakfast instead?" Justin offered.

"Now that sounds more my style this morning," Kiel said, arranging his cap with his good hand.

"You coming?" Justin said, turning casually to Katie. She nodded with a smile, then followed the boys onto the deck by the trailer.

"What was that?" Kiel asked as a loud noise filled the air around them.

Justin turned and looked out into the thick bush that surrounded the campground. He flinched as the sound of snapping branches once again came from amongst the trees.

"Bears," he muttered. It was a sound that Justin had heard many times in the past. He usually heard it when some careless camper had left food or garbage lying outside on the ground. The scent quickly attracted the black bears that lived in the area. Justin knew this could be an extremely dangerous situation and he motioned for his friends to remain still as the sound of breaking branches continued.

Justin peered into the woods. At first he saw nothing, but then he saw something moving a few metres away. A mop of curly black hair and denim flashed between two black pine trees. A flash of silver studs glinted as they caught the morning sunshine.

Recognition flickered across Justin's face as he watched the intruder make his hasty retreat.

"Do you see who I see?" Justin asked.

"That was the kid from the cafe yesterday," Kiel said.

"Yeah, Blackie," Justin said, remembering the name that had been tattooed on the boy's wrist.

"What's he doing in here?" Katie wondered aloud.

"Beats me. But I intend to find out," Justin answered. "You stay here," he told Kiel and Katie as he ran into the bush.

He rushed headlong through the trees, trying to keep one eye on the retreating boy and one on the snapping tree limbs.

Seconds later, Justin was sprawled on the ground, his foot tangled in a mass of willows. He watched helplessly as the boy sped like a jack-rabbit out of sight.

"Great!" Justin seethed as he stood up, and pulled his foot forcefully from under the root that had tripped him. He gazed around swiftly, but Blackie had disappeared.

Anger swelled in his chest as he began to trace his path back through the trees. A glint of red caught the sun amid the endless greenery and Justin paused.

His breath came rapidly as he walked cautiously toward it. The colour drained from his face as he reached out and grasped a large red stained paper that had been impaled on the tree with a slim silver jack-knife.

Justin's hand shook as he unfolded the paper. His breath caught in his throat as he read the words inside: THIS IS YOUR LAST WARNING. FORGET ABOUT THE MONSTER OR ELSE...

The cords of Justin's tension tightened. What in the world was going on, he wondered. He closed the knife, put it in his pocket, and walked slowly back to the trailer.

Kiel and Katie were standing anxiously on the deck when he came back through the bush. His own face was set in a worried frown.

"I lost him," Justin told them with disappointment. "But he left us a parting gift," he added, smoothing out the crumpled sheet for his friends to see.

Kiel took it with his good hand and his eyes grew wide and frightened as he read the words. He handed the paper to Katie and then wiped his hand on his jeans.

Katie handled it reluctantly. She turned pale as she read it as well. She handed it back to Justin with a flourish.

"We'd better show this to our parents and the police," Kiel said. His voice was edged with fear.

"What's the point in that?" Justin asked. "They'll just think it's a sick joke. No, I think it's about time to do a little investigating on our own."

"I guess you're right about telling our parents," Katie agreed. "Even if they do believe it, they'll probably make us stay around the campground all the time. And then we'll never find the answer to this mystery."

The boys nodded their agreement.

"Where do we start then?" Kiel asked.

"Well, first we have to find out who the boy is who left this," Justin answered, holding up the threatening letter.

"Then what?" Katie asked. "It's not like he's going to tell us why he did it."

"Don't worry about that," Justin said. "I have ways of making him talk," he added with a laugh, as he squinted his eyes and pushed his bottom teeth outward like a vampire.

Nervous laughter burst from the group. Justin looked down at the stained paper in his hands and the smile disappeared from his face. Hastily he handed the note to

Katie, who took it as if it were a poison needle. She in turn handed it to Kiel.

An uneasy silence fell as Justin realized that this was no laughing matter. They might be in a great deal of danger and all the laughing in the world wasn't going to change that.

CHAPTER TWELVE

After Justin had hidden the jack-knife and the note under his mattress and a lunch of sandwiches and fruit had been packed, the children set out in search of the mysterious boy.

They were all silent as they walked along the narrow path that led to the beach.

"Where should we start looking?" Katie asked as they came out onto the main road moments later. Once again traffic was thick, and hundreds of people milled around. The morning paper had reported that the creature had been sighted on several occasions in the past days. It appeared that even more people had flocked to Turtle Lake.

"Maybe someone noticed him at the cafe yesterday. I'll check there," Justin suggested, bringing his attention back to Katie's earlier question.

"I'll ask at the gas station and the boat launch," Katie said, her voice filled with excitement.

"I'll keep a lookout at the beach," Kiel said sheepishly.

"Oh, sure," Justin teased. "Take the easy job!"

Justin reached out and affectionately straightened Kiel's crooked cap. It was obvious that he was still stiff and sore from yesterday's accident. He was holding his broken finger close to his chest.

"It's about time you have to do a little work around here," Kiel shot back with a laugh as he re-adjusted his cap to its lopsided position.

"Let's all meet back at the beach in half an hour," Justin said, turning to go to the restaurant. He glanced over his shoulder at Katie and Kiel who were headed to their appointed places.

A group of boys were perched on the stoop in front of the cafe when Justin arrived. He recognized them from yesterday and paused to speak to them.

"Did any of you guys see a kid with black curly hair and a studded jean jacket around here yesterday?" he asked.

"Yeah," a tanned teen-ager said. His brows were knit as if he were trying to recall. "Oh yeah, he was sitting out front here working on a bicycle."

"Oh, I remember him," another boy spoke up. "He was really strange."

"What makes you say that?" Justin asked curiously.

"Well, he did all this fooling around with this bicycle and then he just walked away. I couldn't see exactly what he was doing. He was sort of hunched over the bike like it was some big secret, but I could hear a lot of clanging. Then he just got up and left the bike lying right over there," he said, pointing to a bike stand in front of the cafe.

"We thought he'd forgotten it, so we called out to him," the first teen-ager interjected. "But he didn't answer us. Just took off like there was a pack of wolves at his heels."

Why would the boy leave his bike at the cafe and just walk away, Justin wondered.

"I don't suppose you know who he is?" Justin asked.

"His name must be Kiel," the teen-ager said, looking straight at Justin. "At least that's the name that the little license plate on the back of his bike said."

Justin felt the world spinning around him. Suddenly he understood just what had happened. It was Kiel's bike that the young boy had been tampering with.

Instantly Kiel's strange accident replayed in Justin's head. He could still see Kiel sailing over the handlebars like a rag doll. And then he saw Kiel laying strangely still on the ground.

"Are you okay?" The question broke Justin's train of thought and he looked down at the group who sat on the stoop. "You look kinda white."

"Oh yeah," Justin said smiling wanly. "I'm fine. Thanks a lot for all your help," he said as he turned to leave.

"No problem," he heard one of the boys call out.

He turned and waved good-bye. As he walked slowly toward the beach he recalled the broken bolt. He remembered thinking that the bolt had not been worn away by the passage of time. His legs felt like jelly as he walked along.

CHAPTER THIRTEEN

"Katie!" Justin called out when he saw her coming out of the gas station.

"What's up?" Katie looked concerned at Justin's ashen colour.

"Some boys saw Blackie tampering with Kiel's bike yesterday," he croaked.

"You mean Kiel's accident wasn't an accident after all," Katie gasped in utter disbelief.

Justin nodded.

"But why?"

"I have no idea," Justin admitted. "It just doesn't make any sense. Unless," he paused as an idea began to form in his mind, "unless this was a little reminder of the warning in the poison pen letter."

"But how would he know that we hadn't given up on our investigation?"

"I guess I kind of blurted that out," Justin said with rising colour as he recalled his outburst at Kiel in the restaurant the day before.

Katie nodded her agreement. "We'd better go tell Kiel," she said.

When they got to the beach they saw Kiel motioning to them excitedly. They both broke into a run, weaving in and out of the crush of people on the beach.

"What is it?" Justin asked frantically.

"Look what I spotted," Kiel answered, indicating a familiar denim jacket with silver studs. The jacket was lying no more than three metres away from them on the sand.

"Yeah, but where's the kid that goes with it?" Katie asked anxiously.

Kiel shrugged his shoulders and didn't answer.

Justin, Kiel and Katie began to scan the beach for any signs of Blackie.

People were packed on the beach like sardines. The swimming area was jammed too. It seemed hopeless to Justin. It was almost impossible to find a familiar face in the crowd.

"Let's get out of sight," Justin suggested. "It won't help much if he spots us first."

Kiel and Katie agreed and they all moved off the beach and into the shade of the trees that ringed the outer edges of the beach area.

"There's something I have to tell you," Justin said to Kiel, once they were all seated comfortably.

"What's that?" Kiel asked as he continued to stare at the jean jacket on the sand.

"I think someone was messing around with your bike yesterday," Justin said nervously. He didn't want to alarm his friend.

"What?" Kiel head snapped up. "Who would do such a thing?"

"Him!" Justin motioned to the jacket a few yards away.

"But that's crazy!" Kiel said, looking back and forth from Katie to Justin.

"Tell us about it," Katie said sarcastically.

"Do you think it has anything to do with our investigation of the creature?" Kiel asked.

"I think so," Justin said as he rubbed his forehead. "But I can't understand how."

"I guess we'll just have to wait and see," Kiel said. He clamped his mouth shut and stared at the jacket on the beach.

It seemed as if hours passed before the crowds began to thin. The sun moved higher into the sky and the heat became almost unbearable. Morning slid into afternoon, and still there was no sign of the mysterious boy. Justin, Kiel and Katie finally ate the lunch they had packed and then got more comfortable for the long afternoon ahead.

Katie lay down on her stomach and began looking at the faces of the other people on the beach.

Justin sat quietly against a tree going over in his mind everything that had happened in the past few days. He felt as though he was living a nightmare as he contemplated all the strange events that had taken place.

The unsettling thoughts that flitted through his mind made Justin tired and he leaned back on the grass to get more comfortable. Before long the heat of the sun began to make him drowsy.

Kiel leaned carefully against a tree and watched people milling around on the beach.

It was more than half an hour later when Justin awoke with a start. "Oh, no!" he exclaimed.

Katie looked up, startled. She had been so deep in thought that she had forgotten all about the boy they were looking for.

Kiel sat up with a start and glanced around at the people on the beach.

They all looked at the spot where the jacket had been. The jacket was gone. The boy was nowhere in sight.

"I can't believe I fell asleep," Justin muttered angrily.

"I wish I had been sleeping," Katie said. "At least then I'd have an excuse for not paying attention."

"Now we'll probably never find him," Kiel moaned, then picked up a handful of grass and threw it violently into the air. The rapid movement seemed to jar his aching muscles and he winced in pain.

"We might as well go home. There's no point staying here on the off-chance that he'll come back," Justin said.

Downcast, the children trudged towards the road that led to the campground. None of them spoke.

They were almost at the turnoff that led to the campground when Justin saw Blackie. He was walking no more than ten metres ahead of them, his jacket slung over his shoulder.

"I can't believe the luck," Justin breathed.

"Me, either," Kiel echoed.

"Let's follow him," Justin suggested, the excitement rolling through him.

They were all quiet as they followed the young boy along the winding road.

"Make sure he doesn't see us," Justin hissed, then ducked behind a low row of hedges on the edge of the road. He grabbed Katie by the arm and hauled her in behind him.

Just then, Blackie turned around as if sensing movement behind him. Kiel dived into the hedge at the last moment, barely missing being seen. He gave a grunt of agony as he landed with a thud next to Justin.

"Are you okay?" Katie asked at his pain-filled cry.

"I'll live," Kiel muttered. "At least I think I will." He stood up and rubbed at his sore arms. He held his broken finger close to his chest as he followed Katie and Justin back out onto the beach road.

They continued to nip in and out of the bushes as they followed the dark-haired boy. Luckily, Justin thought, he seemed unaware of their presence.

They had been walking for more than twenty minutes when Blackie finally turned off the road towards a log cabin. The children watched silently as he entered the cabin without knocking and closed the door firmly behind him.

"Now what?" Kiel asked, as they all ducked between two rows of lilac bushes.

"Let's just stay here for a while and see what he does next," Justin suggested.

They crept down further beside the hedge and waited. Several moments passed. Then the cabin door opened and a man came out.

Justin couldn't see the man's face as he walked down to the beach, his back to them. Bending over, the man picked up something and turned back towards the house.

Justin recognized him at once. A shock of bright red hair framed his face.

It was Mr. Lawford, the owner of the Crystal Palace Hotel.

CHAPTER FOURTEEN

"What the heck's going on around here?" Justin said in a hushed whisper. He turned to Katie and Kiel, who were staring at him in confusion.

First, Mr. Lawford and his partner had warned them away from Indian Point. Then came the suspicious boating accident. Then there had been Kiel's unfortunate bike accident, that had been no accident at all. And now, finally, they had discovered the mysterious black-haired boy staying in the same cabin as the owner of the hotel. Something strange was certainly going on, Justin thought. Something very strange indeed.

"I wonder what the connection is between those two?" Katie said, voicing aloud the question that Justin had been silently asking himself.

Justin and Kiel simply shrugged their shoulders.

The three detectives stayed hidden, watching silently as Mr. Lawford went back into the house. The group waited patiently for several moments, but he did not come back outside.

"We'd better get home now," Justin whispered. "Our parents will be getting worried soon." The position of the sun and three growling stomachs proved that it was close to supper-time.

Justin motioned for Katie and Kiel to follow as he crept out from their shelter in the hedge, then ran to the main road a short distance away.

"How do you think those two are involved in this?" Justin asked as they started the long walk home.

"Maybe they saw the creature disappear near Indian Point too," Kiel said, rushing to catch up to Justin who was walking at a rapid pace.

"Yeah, maybe they're investigating the monster themselves and are afraid we'll solve the mystery before they do," Katie said.

"That would explain why Mr. Lawford and Mr. Schmidt warned us about going to Indian Point," Justin said.

"Whoever finally works it all out will be quite famous," Katie said.

"And very rich," Justin said. "Don't forget the $5,000 reward."

The more Justin thought about it, the more sense it made. If Mr. Lawford and Blackie were getting close to discovering the truth, then the children's investigation could be quite a threat. It would certainly explain why they were willing to go to such lengths to keep the trio out of the way.

"We really can't be sure of any of this," Justin mused. "This whole thing is just like one big puzzle."

"With a lot of big pieces missing," Kiel added, sounding more downhearted.

"I guess we'll just have to work a little harder to find the missing pieces," Katie said optimistically. She seemed undeterred by the boys' discouraged tones.

Kiel and Justin looked at Katie and then gave each other a conspiratorial smile.

"Right you are, milady," Justin said with a grand bow.

Katie burst into giggles.

"Where do we start?" she asked enthusiastically after her laughter had subsided.

"Well, I think we should keep an eye on those two," Justin said. He motioned back to the log cabin with the sweep of his arm.

"We could come back first thing in the morning," Katie said with growing excitement.

"Yeah," Kiel said, caught up in his sister's enthusiasm. "We can stake the place out. Just like they do in the movies." A devious grin was forming rapidly at the corners of his mouth.

"Maybe they'll lead us right to the monster," Katie said brightly.

"Or at least to some clues that might help us find out what's going on," Justin said. He too was becoming excited at the prospect of getting to the bottom of the strange events of the past few days.

At least he was excited until Kiel's voice broke his reverie.

"What if we're caught?" he asked, nervousness edging his voice.

"Huh?" Justin asked. The thought hadn't even occurred to him.

"If they catch us spying on them, we could be in a lot of trouble," Kiel warned. "Who knows how far they're willing to go to keep their secrets."

Justin's sense of adventure was dramatically lessened as he pondered the question. How far were these strangers willing to go?

CHAPTER FIFTEEN

"What are you kids planning on doing today?" Kiel's mother asked as they sat down to a breakfast of pancakes and bacon.

"We're just going to hang around at the beach," Kiel answered for his friends.

"Have you decided to give up the detective business, then?" Mr. Daniels asked with a suspicious look at Justin.

"Yeah," Justin answered, then glanced at Katie and Kiel with a knowing look.

"That's good to hear. There's no point in your getting into any more situations," Mr. Daniels said. "At least not until we get to the bottom of this boating accident."

Katie's cheeks had turned a flaming red and Kiel was squirming in his seat uncomfortably. Justin was nervously looking down at his shoes, but his father did not seem to notice.

"You kids run along then," Mrs. Daniels said. "We'll do the dishes today."

"Yahoo!" Justin cheered. He nearly bolted from his seat. He wanted to get out of the trailer as soon as possible. His father's line of questioning was making him uncomfortable. And from the guilty looks on Katie and Kiel's faces they too were feeling like caged animals.

With a quick wave to their parents the group headed out of the campground and on to the main road.

Justin couldn't believe how well all three of them were getting along. He and Katie no longer tried to make each other angry. He didn't know what was behind her sudden change of heart. She hardly ever tried to cause an argument. Justin didn't know how long the peace would last but decided to relax and enjoy it while it did.

Before long Justin could see the log cabin off in the distance. He motioned for Katie and Kiel to walk close to the hedges as they drew nearer.

"This way," Justin whispered when they were only a few metres from the yard. He gestured for them to follow him as he ducked down beside the trees that lined the road.

Hunching close to the ground, they moved slowly along until they reached the hedges where they had hidden yesterday. They hid between the rows of lilac bushes.

"I think we're safe here," Justin murmured as he sat down on the narrow strip of grass between the rows of greenery.

Katie and Kiel took up places next to him. Each of them turned to look at the log cabin through the bright green growth of the lilac bush.

Justin had rarely been near the beach in the early morning hours. He was surprised that the normal rush of traffic was absent. There was no laughter ringing through the air, or boats racing across the lake. The noises nearby seemed more distinct, like the sound of an occasional car passing by and the beautiful lilt of a robin singing off in the distance.

The sound of a door opening and then slamming shut broke the silence of the morning. Justin and his friends strained to see between the branches of the hedge.

Justin was the first to spot Blackie pacing back and forth across the yard. It was obvious that he was very upset about something. He was angrily kicking at the ground, sending clods of earth spinning into the air. He was muttering under his breath, but Justin could not make out a word that he was saying.

Justin signalled for Katie and Kiel to sit perfectly still, placing his finger over his lips, then pointing to the boy in the yard. Katie and Kiel nodded.

Blackie seemed unaware of their presence. He finally stopped pacing and flopped down on the cabin steps. A few minutes passed before the door opened and closed for a second time. This time Mr. Lawford came out.

Justin strained to hear as Blackie began to speak.

"It isn't right what you're doing, Dad," he said angrily.

"I already told you, it's none of your business anyway," the red-haired man replied. His voice was menacing and thick with anger. Without another word he turned and walked to a boat-house that sat on the lake in front of the cabin.

Justin had never seen a boat-house quite as fancy as this one. Unlike the hundreds of others dotting the shore of Turtle Lake, this one was completely covered in except for one single small window. The building was painted a bright canary yellow.

"Where did he go?" Kiel whispered when the man moved out of his range of vision.

"He went into that boat-house over there." Justin pointed slowly to the yellow building nearby.

Just then Blackie stood up and moved towards the hedge, the same hedge that hid Kiel, Justin and Katie. Justin closed his hand over Kiel's mouth and gave Katie a silencing look.

"Oh, no!" Katie rasped, "we've been caught." She clamped her mouth shut. Justin's body tensed.

When Blackie was no more than a metre from the hedge, he bent down. Justin held his breath as the boy's face came frighteningly close to his own, separated only by the thickness of the hedge.

Glancing down, Justin saw a bright red ball nearly hidden beneath a pile of recently cut grass. He sat motionless as the boy picked up the ball, stood up, turned, and walked to the road.

Justin heaved a sigh of relief.

"Boy, that was close," he said breathlessly as the sound of running shoes crunching on gravel faded away.

"It sure was," Kiel and Katie said in unison.

Still crouching low behind the hedge, Justin turned his attention back to the boat-house. The building was still strangely silent.

No boats had left the building. For that matter, Justin thought, neither had Mr. Lawford.

Justin began to grow restless as time began to tick slowly by. First fifteen minutes, then half an hour, then finally an hour. Kiel was struggling to get comfortable beside him, and Katie was muttering about the branches from the lilac bushes snagging her hair.

"What in the world could he be doing in there?" she complained.

"Are you sure he didn't go back into the house already?" Kiel asked Justin.

"No way," Justin said adamantly. He was certain that he would have seen the man if he had crossed the yard to the house.

"Maybe he left in a boat," Katie suggested with a restless twitch.

"We would have heard the boat," Justin replied. The early morning silence had yet to be broken by the sounds of a boat motor.

"Let's go have a peek in the window," Katie said bravely.

"Are you kidding?" Kiel whispered hoarsely.

"Well, it's better than sitting here for the rest of our lives," Katie shot back irritably.

"Once we leave here," Kiel protested, "they can easily see us."

"It's a chance we have to take," Justin broke in. It looked as though Katie and Kiel were going to come to blows soon. They were staring at each other angrily.

Kiel glanced at Justin in amazement, then nodded his head in reluctant agreement.

Slowly Justin crept from their shelter in the trees, with Katie close behind. Kiel moved hesitantly behind them. Once they reached the boat-house they slid their backs against the bright yellow wall until they came to the window.

With their heads pressed tightly together they peeked into the building. It took several seconds for Justin's eyes to adjust to the darkness inside. Finally everything came into focus. He stiffened as if he'd been dealt a physical blow.

"What do you see?" Katie asked in a hushed whisper. She was vying for a small area of window to peek in.

Justin stepped away from the window and let Katie look inside. Her face was a mask of surprise as she turned back to Justin.

"The building's empty," Kiel said, turning with amazement to the other two.

"But that's impossible," Katie said, then peeked in again. It was almost as though she did not trust her own eyes, Justin thought.

"It may be impossible," Justin said. "But it is empty!"

He looked at Kiel and Katie in astonishment. There was simply no way that a boat could have left the building without being seen or heard.

"Just what do you think you're doing?" a voice boomed out behind them.

Justin barely had time to understand what was going on before a large hand grasped his shoulder. The fingers dug in painfully as he turned towards the angry sound. It was Herb Schmidt from the Crystal Palace Hotel. A look of fury darkened his face.

Justin, Katie and Kiel backed away, but came to a painful stop when their backs met the unyielding wall of the boathouse.

The man took an intimidating step towards them.

They were trapped.

Chapter sixteen

To Justin, it felt as if time was standing still, as he and his friends stood, trapped, against the boat-house wall. The face of the angry old man grimaced down at them.

Justin looked around desperately for a way to escape, but there was none.

The sudden sound of a vehicle on the beach road drew Justin's attention and he glanced to his right. Just then the green side of a half-ton truck became visible. Justin's eyes snapped back to the old man who held them captive and saw that the appearance of the truck had caught him off guard as well. He pulled his hands to his sides as the driver of the truck glanced their way.

The truck disappeared around a turn in a moment, but it was all the time that Justin needed.

"Run," he screamed as he bolted out of reach of the angry man, shoving a startled Katie along with him.

Kiel tried to run as well, but his steps were slowed by his stiff body, and he was quickly captured in Herb Schmidt's firm grasp. Justin spun around as anger boiled up inside of him. He jumped on the old man's foot with all of his strength.

Schmidt let out a strangled yelp, hobbling on one foot as a string of angry expletives rushed out of him.

Justin wasted no time. He grabbed Kiel by the arm and propelled him toward Katie who had already reached the main road.

"I'm not done with you yet!" an angry shout broke from behind them, but they continued to run. They did not slow their pace until the angry shouts were a mere whisper in the distance.

The sound of a horn tooting nearby sent Justin, Kiel and Katie skittering to the edge of the road. Was Mr. Schmidt still hot on their trail?

Justin spun around, then froze like a deer caught in a beam of light. He let out his breath in a whoosh as he saw the blue of an approaching police car.

"Well, if it isn't our super sleuths," Officer Olsen said as he pulled the car to a stop on the edge of the road. Justin, Kiel and Katie approached the car, still breathless from their escape.

"What are you three doing way out here?" the policeman asked.

"Not much," Justin answered breathlessly.

"Just out for a walk," Katie added, clasping her hands tightly together.

"Looks more like a run," Officer Olsen said with a laugh.

Justin's cheeks were red, and sweat was rolling freely from his forehead. Kiel and Katie looked equally exhausted.

"I guess you could say that," Kiel piped up with a knowing look at Justin.

The officer didn't seem to notice their agitation. "I was on my way over to the campground to see your father," he told them. "How would you like a ride?"

"Great!" Justin cheered. The farther they got away from the old man the better, Justin thought. All ideas of further spying were now gone. He had had enough excitement for one day.

The trip back to the campground was an exciting one. None of the children had ever been in a police car, and their questions were endless.

Officer Olsen laughed as they asked questions about everything from the two-way radio to the nightstick that lay on the seat beside him.

Finally the car came to a halt in front of the Daniels's trailer.

"I'll come around and open the doors for you," the policeman said as Justin searched for a handle in the back door. "There aren't any handles back there," he explained as he stepped out of the car.

"Now you know what it feels like to be a prisoner," he said as he opened the door and the children piled out in a rush.

"More than you'll ever know," Justin muttered. He turned and looked at Katie and Kiel who nodded in agreement.

Justin's heart was still hammering in his chest as he thought how close they had come to becoming prisoners of the angry old man at the cabin.

The three children were just thanking Officer Olsen for the ride when Mr. Roland and Mr. Daniels came out of the trailer.

"What have these kids been up to?" Mr. Daniels asked the police officer with a worried look.

"Nothing criminal, I assure you," the policeman answered. There was a hint of humour in his voice.

"That's good to hear," Mr. Daniels said, relieved.

"I was on my way over to see you when I bumped into the children. I offered them a ride. I hope you don't mind?" Officer Olsen asked.

"Not at all," Mr. Daniels said. "I'm just glad to hear that they were not in any sort of trouble." He looked almost gratefully at Justin. Then he turned and looked seriously at the policeman. "Now what was it you wanted to speak to me about?"

Katie and the boys, who were just about to go into the trailer, stopped to listen.

"We did a little investigating on that poison pen letter. And we found that the fingerprints were small enough to be a child's. Because of that, we've decided that it was more than likely just a prank. So we don't feel there's anything to worry about."

"That's great news," Mr. Daniels said.

"You haven't received any more, have you?" Officer Olsen asked.

"No, not that I know of," Justin's father answered. Then he turned to Justin.

"You haven't got any more of those letters, have you, son?" he asked.

"No, Dad," Justin lied. He didn't want his father to worry. His stomach felt sick, though. He hated lying to his parents. Deep down inside, he wanted to tell his father everything, starting with the second threatening letter, to the recent spying mission. But so much had happened that he didn't even know where to start.

Justin turned and slipped into the trailer, with Katie and Kiel close behind. The men's voices faded into silence. The trailer was quiet except for the gentle purr of the air conditioner.

Their ordeal was over. Justin and Kiel flopped down on the couch while Katie sat in the old rocker.

"I've never been so scared in my whole life," Justin declared with relief.

"Same here," Katie said. She raised her trembling hands in front of her face.

"If that truck hadn't come when it did. . ." Justin's voice trailed off.

"And if you hadn't stomped on old man Schmidt's foot. . ." Kiel smiled thankfully.

"I hate to think what would have happened," Katie added shuddering.

Justin's heart beat faster at the thought.

"Do you think he'll come after us?" Katie asked with renewed worry in her voice.

"I don't think so," Justin answered. But he was filled with doubt.

"What's next then?" Katie asked. "When do we go spy on them again?" She was looking at Justin.

Justin and Kiel looked at her with their mouths hanging open.

"Are you kidding?" Kiel asked.

"Don't you think we've got in enough trouble already?" Justin asked.

"Oh, come on, guys! You're not chickening out on me, are you?" Katie taunted. "Let's go back tonight."

Justin looked at her with a shocked expression. He didn't know whether to laugh or cry. It was obvious that she had

98

every intention of getting to the bottom of the mystery—no matter what. He began to wonder whom he should fear most: Lawford and Schmidt, or Katie.

"Okay. We'll go back tonight," Justin said reluctantly. His stomach was twisted in knots.

"Have you gone nuts?" Kiel asked with a wide-eyed stare.

"I think I must have," Justin answered.

Katie just smiled.

CHAPTER SEVENTEEN

"We're home," Mrs. Daniels called out as she and Mrs. Roland came into the living room, balancing several bags of groceries in their arms.

She stopped in the doorway and looked curiously at Justin.

"What's up?" she asked.

"Oh, nothing, Mom," Justin said, shaking off his fearful thoughts. He imagined that his face was probably pale and frightened looking. The thought of going back to spy on the residents of the log cabin had jarred his nerves.

He tried to feign a bright smile as he stood up to help his mother with the grocery bags.

"What's for supper, Mom?" he asked, trying to change the subject. He knew that if his mother suspected any trouble at all she would be worried sick. And she wouldn't let him out of her sight. There was no way they would be able to unravel the mystery of the monster with his mother watching their every move.

"We're going to barbecue hamburgers tonight," Mrs. Daniels answered. The worried look was now gone from her face.

"All right!" Justin said, his stomach growling.

By the time supper was finished hours later and the dishes cleared away, Justin was feeling better. He had shoved Lawford and Herb Schmidt to the back of his mind, refusing to let the puzzling mystery ruin his day.

"Can we go for a bike ride?" he asked his parents who were now immersed in a game of gin rummy.

Deep down Justin hoped they would say no. If they didn't, the young detectives would have to go through with their plans to return to the log cabin on a spying mission.

Justin's heart sank as his father replied, "Sure, son." He laid down his winning rummy hand with a shout of glee.

"But be back before dark," Mrs. Roland added, as she muttered about being caught with so many points.

Justin and his friends slipped out almost unnoticed as their parents continued the card game.

The air had cooled as the three friends set out. Kiel rode his bike with extra caution as the group headed out to the main road. His father had repaired it before supper and it was now running smoothly. Yet Justin could tell that Kiel was nervous.

Justin rode slowly along beside him until Kiel seemed to relax and even started to look as though he was enjoying the ride. Soon they were all speeding to their destination.

As they neared the log cabin Justin slowed down.

"Better find a place to stash our bikes," he said in hushed tones. Then he glanced around for some place that was close enough to get to in case of an emergency, but far enough away so that they were well hidden.

"Over there," Kiel said, pointing to a small bluff of trees on the left side of the road.

Justin stepped off his bike and pushed it the short distance to the trees. He shoved his bike into the underbrush, then stepped back so that Katie and Kiel could do the same.

Leaving their bikes securely hidden, they crossed the road and crept to the edge of the clear space around the cabin.

The sound of voices sent Justin and his friends racing for the cover of the lilac bushes.

"It's just the neighbours," Justin assured Kiel and Katie as they hunched down between the fragrant rows of hedges.

"Might as well get comfy then," Kiel said. He held his broken finger close to his chest as he sat down beside Justin.

"Could be a long wait," Katie said as she crouched down beside them.

"I don't think so," Justin said, pointing to the cabin. Katie and Kiel peered out through the thick foliage and saw that Mr. Lawford and Herb Schmidt had just stepped out the front door and were now walking into the yard.

Justin heard Katie's sharp intake of breath and he glanced at her. She looked frightened. He gave her a reassuring smile, then put his finger to his lips.

Kiel and Katie relaxed and sat silently watching.

Justin tried to force his own fear from his thoughts. The frightening incident of the morning played over repeatedly in his mind.

From their hiding place in the hedges, Justin watched as the men built a fire in a pit less than five metres away. At first, nothing but a huge cloud of grey smoke rose from the pit. The cloud sailed across the yard and engulfed the hedges. Justin's eyes began to burn and he turned to see if his friends were also being affected. Kiel had tears running down his face. Katie had her hands firmly pressed against her eyes in a futile attempt to block out the horrible smoke.

It was only with a great deal of self-control that Justin kept from coughing. Finally, flames began to lick at the wood and the smoke disappeared as fire engulfed the slabs of birch.

Justin took huge gulps of fresh air as he watched Mr. Lawford walk back to the cabin. Within moments he had returned with two tall drinks. He handed one to Mr. Schmidt.

"Well, here's to the final night of the Turtle Lake Monster," the old man said, raising his glass in a toast.

"May he rest in peace," Mr. Lawford said, smiling broadly.

Both men took a huge swallow and then started to laugh.

"Oh no!" Katie said in a hushed voice. "They're going to kill the monster."

"But why?" Kiel whispered.

"For the reward money, of course," Justin said with disgust. "What better proof that the creature truly exists than the monster itself? Dead or alive."

Justin silenced the others with a gesture as the men's voices rose once more.

"If it wasn't for those snoopy kids we could have kept this up all summer," the old man said angrily.

"Yeah, just imagine the money we could have raked in." Mr. Lawford shook his head.

"I should have done away with the little brats when I had the chance," Herb Schmidt said angrily.

"Well, it'll all be over with by tomorrow night. If they get in our way before then, they'll get what's coming to them." Mr. Lawford gave a cruel laugh.

When the two men finally got up to refill their drinks, Justin motioned to Katie and Kiel that it was time to leave. Once the cabin door had closed behind the two men, the group made a mad dash out from behind the hedges and down the main road.

"What do you think they meant when they said if it wasn't for us they could have kept this up all summer?" Kiel asked.

"They probably meant that they could have kept the location of the creature's home a secret until the reward money went up," Justin said.

"That's probably it. The amount of the reward would have kept going up as the summer went on," Katie agreed.

"Do you really think they're going to kill the creature tomorrow?" Katie asked. Her voice was full of worry.

"Not if there's anything that I can do about it," Justin replied angrily.

Justin frowned as he tried to decide what to do.

When he spoke a moment later, his voice was firm.

"Tomorrow we're going to get a boat and go over to Indian Point," he told his friends. "There must be something there that we missed the last time. Some clue that will lead us to the creature."

"It's our only chance to stop them," Katie admitted.

"But remember what they said they'd do if we got in their way tomorrow," Kiel warned.

"That's a chance we'll just have to take," Justin said. His words left no room for argument.

"But we could be kidnapped or. . . or. . ." Kiel said with a gulp.

"Or worse!" Justin finished for him.

CHAPTER EIGHTEEN

Justin awoke early the next morning. Already the air felt hot and dry. Since his parents were still asleep, he dressed as quietly as he could and slipped from the trailer.

Justin ran across the yard to the Rolands' tent and knelt down beside the window.

"Psst, Katie, Kiel, wake up," he whispered.

He waited several moments before Kiel's sleepy face peered out through the screened window.

"What do you want?" he asked. His voice was still thick with sleep.

"Let's get going," Justin whispered. "We've got a lot of stuff to do today." He looked at Kiel impatiently. He didn't want to have to remind Kiel that they were going to search for the monster, just in case his parents might be listening.

Kiel's face brightened with the recollection. "I'll be out in a minute."

Justin watched anxiously as Kiel replaced the tarp over the window. Seconds later, he could hear muffled voices inside the tent. Finally, after what seemed like hours, Kiel and Katie emerged from the tent fully dressed.

Katie's hair was sticking up in every direction, and she still looked half asleep.

When they arrived at the shower house moments later, she disappeared into the women's washroom. When she came out a few minutes later, her hair had been combed and her face was freshly scrubbed.

They all joined forces to do the morning chores, but the job was slow going. The early morning heat was oppressive.

"How are we going to get to the point?" Kiel asked as he scrubbed the sink.

"I asked Dad if we could use the campground canoe," Justin said as he polished the row of mirrors to a gloss.

"That's one good thing," Katie muttered. "You wouldn't get me in another paddle-boat if my life depended on it."

"Let's go then," Justin said as he cleaned the last of the mirrors. He grabbed the pail and mop and led the other two outside.

Once they had stored the supplies in the tool shed they started across the campground to where the canoe was stored.

Anxiety was pressing in on Justin as they carried the canoe to the beach. But no matter how frightened he felt, he knew that there was no turning back now. He had to try to stop Mr. Lawford and Mr. Schmidt from killing the creature. Going to Indian Point in search of clues appeared to be their only hope.

It seemed to take forever to lug the cumbersome canoe to the beach. The oppressive heat slowed their pace and did little to cheer their spirits. Justin's face was set in a permanent frown when they finally arrived.

The beach was already jammed with people. It seemed that all the new sightings of the creature had only served to stir up extra excitement. The newspapers were filled with accounts of recent sightings. The creature had been seen on more than fifteen occasions in the past two days.

Justin ignored the hubbub around him and led the group to the water's edge. Once they had fastened their life-jackets and pushed the canoe out into the waters of the lake, the air began to cool. Sea-gulls dipped headlong into the water for their morning prey. The call of the loons echoed from shore to shore.

The canoe ride across the lake took more than an hour. As the cliffs of the point rose in the distance, Justin paddled faster. He felt increasingly tense as the sheer rock walls came into view.

Justin brought the canoe to a halt when the cliffs were near enough to reach out and touch.

"What exactly are we looking for?" Kiel asked.

"I really don't know," Justin answered. "But I guess we'll know when we see it."

Slowly paddling the canoe, they rounded the sides of the cliff. Both boys and Katie scanned the vine-covered walls for clues.

"Wait... look at that," Justin yelled excitedly as he stopped paddling and pointed high above his head.

"Look at what?" Kiel asked, shifting his gaze upward.

"Up there, by the tree root," Justin said impatiently.

"The tree root!" Katie muttered. "The whole cliff is covered with tree roots."

Justin stared at her in exasperation. "There," he hissed, jabbing his finger repeatedly towards something green and scaly—like the skin a snake sheds, only larger. This piece was the size of a large handkerchief.

"Are there snakes that big around here?" Katie asked as she caught sight of whatever it was. She shuddered involuntarily.

"No way," Justin assured her.

"What is it then?" Kiel asked. He sat gazing at the odd green object.

"Got me beat," Justin said. "Help me up." He stood up and balanced one foot on each side of the canoe. The canoe began to pitch violently from side to side, threatening to send all three of them into the water.

"Be careful!" Kiel yelled, reaching out to steady one of Justin's legs. Katie in turn steadied Justin's other leg. The canoe settled down to a gentle rocking.

The strange piece of skin was still out of reach as Justin extended his arms over his head.

"Hold on tight!" Justin shouted as he pitched himself upward. His hand had just grasped the clammy skin when he felt the boat lurch sideways.

"Oh no!" he cried as he grabbed at a handful of vines to steady himself.

Everything seemed to slow down as Justin lost his footing and fell from the canoe. His body hurtled towards the cliff, his hand still gripping the strong vines.

Suddenly there was complete darkness. The vines parted like a giant mouth and swallowed him up.

CHAPTER NINETEEN

It took several moments for Justin's eyes to focus in the darkness. He knew he was in deep water. He couldn't touch bottom. His life-jacket was keeping his head from dipping beneath the surface of the water.

As his eyes adjusted he began to look carefully at his surroundings. He was in some sort of cave. He appeared to be floating in a pool in the center of a circular stone cavern. A narrow ledge less than a metre wide rimmed the side of the cave. Turning around, he saw the wall of vines which hung like a curtain, disguising the entrance to the cave.

Suddenly everything became clear to Justin. He knew that this was where the creature had disappeared. It had not submerged in the shallow waters surrounding the point. Instead it had merely forced its way through the wall of vines into the cavern.

Justin was still clutching the clammy piece of green skin tightly in his hand. He brought it up to examine the material more closely, but it was almost impossible to see in the darkness of the cave.

Justin was almost certain that the skin must have been torn off the creature as it had pushed its way into the cave.

Panic overtook him as he also realized that the creature could return at any moment. He swam frantically for the ledge, and dragged himself up onto the rocky lip. Then he lay back on the cold stony surface trying to catch his breath.

The silence in the cavern was suddenly shattered. Justin could hear the muffled voices of Kiel and Katie calling out his name. They echoed around the cave.

"Justinnnn," Kiel's frantic voice filtered in.

"I'm in here!" Justin called out.

"Where's here?" Kiel asked, relieved.

"I'm inside a cave behind the vines," Justin answered.

"How do we get there?" Katie shouted.

"Tie the canoe to the rocks and swim to the vines. You should be able to pull them far enough apart to come through. The bottom of the cave is under water so you can swim right in. But keep your life-jackets on, it's really deep in here," he warned.

"We're on our way," Kiel called.

Justin leaned against the cave wall taking in the strange beauty of this quiet place as he waited for his friends.

Suddenly a crack of light shone into the cave, as the vines parted to allow Katie and Kiel to enter.

"Wow! Would you look at this place," Kiel said excitedly as he swam inside.

A broad smile brightened Katie's face as she splashed towards the slippery ledge where Justin now sat.

Justin helped them onto the ledge which was now slick from their wet clothing.

"What do you suppose made this cave?" Kiel asked, gazing around in wonder. He was holding his arm close to his chest. The bandage on his finger was dripping wet.

"It's probably been here for millions of years. The water slapping against the rocks could have eaten it away gradually," Katie answered.

"I wonder if we're the first people to ever be in here," Kiel said wistfully.

"We may be the first people," Justin said, "but not the first living creatures, I'll bet."

"What do you mean?" Katie asked. Then her eyes opened into huge round circles as understanding flickered across her face. Quickly she pulled her legs close to her body and away from the water that lapped at the ledge.

"You mean you think this is where the creature lives," Kiel whispered. He too pulled his legs up to his chest.

Justin just nodded. The cave fell silent.

The stillness was broken moments later when the cavern was filled with a deafening roar of splashing water. The water began to roll and bubble like a pot of stew on a blazing fire. Foam spewed onto the ledge.

Justin watched in horror as light filtered into the cave. The vines were slowly parting as something pushed its way up from beneath them, and into the cave.

"Oh, no," Katie cried out. She stood up and backed tightly against the cave wall.

"What is it?" Kiel squealed as he scrambled to a standing position.

"It's the creature!" Justin bellowed. His feet slipped on the slick ledge as he stood up as well.

The water continued to roll in front of them as the creature began to rise up to the surface of the bubbling pool.

"Hide!" Justin shouted as his eyes scanned the dimly lit cave.

"Over there," Kiel called and started to run for a small rock pile further along the ledge.

Justin's feet skidded along the slippery rock as he followed. He froze as he heard Katie cry out. He spun around
just as Katie lost her footing and started to slip into the water
below.

Justin raced back, his own feet sliding dangerously close
to the edge. Katie was already beginning to sink into the
frothing pool.

He grabbed the back of her life-jacket and hauled her
back onto the ledge with a grunt.

Her face was a sickly pale colour as she scrambled on
her hands and knees to where her brother was hiding.

Justin crouched with Katie and Kiel behind the safety of
the pile of rocks as the creature came to rest near the surface
of the water. The vines dropped back into place behind it.
Once again the cavern was cast into a grey-black gloom.

As Justin's eyes once again adjusted to the darkness he
noticed that the cave no longer seemed as large. The huge
beast swallowed up the space with its massive bulk. Justin
felt a chill as he wondered whether or not the creature had
seen them.

The legendary beast's black eyes stared straight at the
rock pile where they now hid. Its head was huge. Its skin
was blackish-green and looked almost like rubber. Yet it
was not shiny or slippery looking.

Justin held his breath, waiting for the first signs of attack.

CHAPTER TWENTY

Justin felt as though he was trapped in a place where time did not exist. He waited in horror for the creature to attack. Each moment seemed to pass with painful slowness.

An eerie hush had descended as the creature rested immobile in the cave pool. Not even a flicker of movement was visible from their hiding place behind the rocks. Suddenly a high-pitched metallic scream burst from the beast. Justin, Kiel and Katie strained forward to see what had caused the creature to make the terrible noise.

To Justin's surprise, the creature's head was not thrown back in an agonizing cry as he had expected. Instead it remained completely still. Not even its cold black eyes moved. A gasp of horror escaped Justin's throat as the stomach of the beast began to heave. He watched, startled, as the side of the creature began to swell. As first it moved out slowly. Then suddenly the beast's skin opened up. It was a door.

Justin, Kiel and Katie gaped at each other. Katie appeared in shock. Kiel and Justin looked at each other in total disbelief. The creature was not alive. In fact, Justin realized, it was nothing more than an elaborately decorated submarine.

"It's a hoax," Katie sputtered.

"Quiet," Justin said. He hunched down as far as he could to watch, as two figures emerged from the side of the incredible fraud. They were Lawford and Herb Schmidt, the owners of the Crystal Palace Hotel.

They stepped out of the elaborate machine and onto the ledge on the opposite side of the cave. As they stood admiring their creation they began to laugh.

"I hate to dismantle our brilliant money maker," Mr. Lawford said, patting the monster on the head. His red hair looked eerie in the semi-darkness of the cave.

"One more trip across the lake to the boat-house and then it'll all be over with," Herb Schmidt said sadly.

"Not to worry, my friend," the red-haired man retorted. "By tonight everyone on the lake will be talking about the creature."

"After the monster's final journey today there won't be a soul who doesn't believe in his existence," the old man said triumphantly. "He'll be a legend. And we'll be raking money in at the hotel for years to come. Every gullible tourist in the country will come to Turtle Lake in hopes of seeing the beast," the old man said, rubbing his hands together.

Mr. Lawford nodded in agreement. Both men began to laugh.

Suddenly, Justin recalled how Mr. Lawford had disappeared in the boat-house. With a bolt of understanding he realized that he had not disappeared at all. He had simply left the building in the submarine, so that Justin and his friends could neither hear nor see his departure.

Mr. Lawford's booming voice pulled Justin out of the past and drew his attention back to the two men on the ledge. He held his breath as he listened to them talk.

"Let's go then. News travels fast around Turtle Lake. After our last little run across the lake there should be hundreds of people crowding onto the beaches to see if the creature returns," Lawford said.

"Yeah, we'll give everyone a show they won't forget for the rest of their lives. Then we'll dismantle our masterpiece at the boat-house and burn all the evidence," Herb Schmidt said happily. Both men turned and went back inside the submarine. The door closed behind them with a solid thud.

Justin felt disgust overwhelm him. It appeared that Lawford and Schmidt were only biding their time in the cave so they could ensure a large crowd for their final appearance. They had probably attracted the attention of hundreds with their earlier trip across the lake.

"Oh no! What are we going to do?" Katie's hoarse whisper broke Justin's train of thought.

"Once they dismantle it we won't have any proof of what those men have done," Justin blurted out as panic rose in his voice. He knew that they would have to act fast if they were going to stop the men before it was too late. His mind worked frantically to formulate a plan. Suddenly he knew what had to be done.

"You go get help. Take the canoe along the shore until you get to a cabin. There are a whole bunch of them close by," he told his friends. Then he turned and jumped into the cave pool. "Get to a phone and call the police. Tell them to get over to the boat-house!" he shouted as he swam frantically towards the submarine.

"But what are you going to do?" Kiel asked, panic-stricken.

"I'm going with them," Justin called, as the cave filled up with a now familiar bubbling roar. Justin pulled himself onto the back of the mechanical beast, undoing his life-jacket and heaving it into the water as he placed his arms firmly around its neck.

"No!" Kiel and Katie screamed.

"You'll be drowned," Katie added, horrified.

Her words fell on deaf ears. Justin knew that wearing the life- jacket was no use if he was going to succeed. Already the creature was disappearing below the surface of the water. Justin's arms and legs were wrapped around the mechanical monster's neck in a death grip. Within seconds Justin was below the surface of the water. Now only the head of the beast was visible as it pushed its way back through the wall of vines and out into Turtle Lake.

CHAPTER TWENTY-ONE

Justin thought his chest would burst. He didn't know how much longer he could hold his breath. His lungs were screaming out for air and his arms were beginning to feel weak as the submarine moved under the wall of vines. Suddenly, just as he felt that he could hold on no longer, the creature began to rise upward toward the lake's surface. Justin held on with the last of his strength as the massive machine broke the surface of the lake. They were now outside the cave.

He felt dizzy as he gasped for breath. The fresh summer air had never felt so good and his lungs fought to refresh themselves.

Suddenly Justin caught a glimpse of the canoe out of the corner of his eye. It was tied to a small outcropping of rock to the right of the cave mouth. He glanced toward it as panic rose in his chest. What would happen if the men in the submarine spotted it as well? He held his breath, waiting to see if they would come to a sudden stop.

His heartbeat and breathing returned to normal as the elaborately disguised machine finally moved past the small canoe and out onto the lake. It was obvious that the submarine's view was not peripheral. Its vision seemed to be limited by a periscope that must be located in the neck of the beast. The men inside the submarine did not seem to be aware of the presence of the small craft.

As the submarine began its final lazy journey across the lake, Justin began to analyze the predicament he was in. His only hope was Katie and Kiel. It was vitally important that they get to help in time. He didn't even want to think about what would happen if he and the men inside the submarine arrived at the boat-house before the police.

He now knew what the hotel owners were capable of doing. He shuddered to think about what would happen if he was caught clinging to the neck of the giant hoax.

He began to relax as the submarine rolled slowly across the lake. He could see people on the beach in the distance, but they were too far away for him to see their faces. He wondered if they were watching the monster's slow progress across the lake.

The submarine dipped beneath the surface once again when a fishing boat headed in its direction. Justin waved frantically at the boat's occupants, but he didn't know whether they had seen him or not. The sub submerged and then came back up after a short distance.

It seemed to Justin that the men inside the submarine were in no hurry. The ride across the lake was a leisurely one. It was as if they wanted everyone at Turtle Lake to see the creature's final appearance.

At last Justin saw the bright yellow boat-house in the distance. He panicked as he felt the machine beneath him begin to descend. He knew he could not hold his breath underwater until they arrived at the boat-house. It was still several hundred metres away.

Justin knew that the situation was bleak. But he also knew that he had to try. If Katie and Kiel had not been able to get help, then it would be up to him to stop the men from destroying the elaborate hoax. This was the only evidence that existed to prove that the creature was nothing more than a fraud.

As the submarine again sank below the surface, Justin held on with all of his strength. He took one huge final breath of air before the water rose above his head.

The water beneath the surface tore at Justin's arms as the submarine moved slowly towards the boat-house. Seaweed slapped in his face as they got closer to the shore. His lungs screamed for air. Great sparks of light exploded in his head.

It was hopeless. Justin's arms were now so weak he could no longer hold on. He released his grip on the mechanical creature and began to struggle frantically for the surface.

"I'm going to drown," Justin thought, just before blackness surrounded him.

Moments later, a painful white light tore at Justin's eyes. It was as if someone had taken a hundred-watt light bulb and placed it close to his eyes.

At first, his mind was utterly confused. He couldn't understand where he was or why he was there. Within seconds his thoughts began to clear and the world around him came into focus. He was bobbing on the surface of Turtle Lake. The sun was shining brightly in his face.

Dizziness overtook him again, and he began to do a desperate dog paddle as his eyes scanned the shore. He was only a few feet from the bright yellow boat-house. He knew that the men would now be inside.

He pulled himself up onto the shore and lay back. He had nearly drowned. But he couldn't think about that now.

He had to stop Lawford and Schmidt from destroying the evidence.

It took all of his strength to pull himself to his feet. His sopping wet clothes were heavy and uncomfortable as he made his way along the side of the boat-house to the building's only door.

As his hand closed over the doorknob he felt his legs begin to buckle. He was exhausted. His body began to fall forward, but he was helpless to stop the motion. The door swung open as his legs turned to jelly and gave way beneath him.

He collapsed half-in and half-out of the building. As darkness began to envelop him once more, he wondered whether his mind was playing tricks on him or whether he was dreaming. For there on the walkaway that surrounded the inside of the building stood Officer Olsen with Mr. Lawford and Herb Schmidt beside him. Their hands appeared to be tightly bound in shiny metal handcuffs. Justin was sure he was imagining things when he also saw Kiel and Katie. Everything went black.

CHAPTER TWENTY-TWO

When Justin came to several moments later, he was lying on the grass outside the boat-house and there was a rush of activity going on around him. Katie and Kiel and Officer Olsen were hovering over him. Out of the corner of his eye, Justin could see another officer loading Mr. Lawford and Herb Schmidt into a nearby police car.

"I'm okay," Justin mumbled to Katie and Kiel who were looking down at him with deep concern. His voice was barely audible. He tried to sit up but his head felt like a watermelon.

"Relax son," Officer Olsen said, putting a soothing hand on Justin's forehead. "It's going to be okay."

Justin made an effort to smile. It was all over. The mystery had been solved. He laid his head back on the green grass and relaxed.

The next few hours were a blur in his mind. The world went by in a rush around him. He had only images of police cars and ambulances, hospital hallways and family.

Justin slept that night like a newborn baby.

The next morning Justin was sitting on the couch, now fully recovered from yesterday's ordeal.

"Look at this," Katie said excitedly as she came into the Daniels's trailer, waving a newspaper in her hand.

Everyone gathered around as Justin took the paper from Katie and spread it out on his lap. Everyone roared with laughter at the picture on the front page. Beneath the heading YOUNG DETECTIVES CRACK CASE OF THE TURTLE LAKE MONSTER, was a picture of Justin riding on the creature's back. He was waving his arms in the air. The photo had been taken by someone in the fishing boat that Justin had seen yesterday.

Justin read the story beneath the picture out loud for his family and friends. It told how the children had discovered the cave and then uncovered the plans of the hotel owners. The story went on to say that the culprits had admitted to getting the idea for the creature after discovering the cave at Indian Point.

Herb Schmidt, who had been a submarine expert in the navy, had designed the elaborate hoax. Both men admitted that the hoax was meant to bring in a lot of business to their failing hotel and boat rentals office. They had added, with bragging tones, that it had certainly done that. Unfortunately they wouldn't be around to enjoy their money for quite some time, Justin thought. Both men were now in police custody and several charges had been laid against them.

Lawford and Schmidt had also admitted to tampering with the paddle-boat—though they added that they had only wanted to frighten the children, not harm them. Justin now realized that the men must have cut the line to the paddle-wheels while he and his friends had been in the restaurant.

"It says here," Justin said, looking at Kiel, "that Mr. Lawford and Herb Schmidt were wanted by the police in Ontario."

"What for?" Kiel asked.

Justin quickly scanned the article before he spoke. "It seems they pulled some scam in Toronto. It says here," he pointed to the newspaper, "that they duped several investors out of millions of dollars."

"Wow," Katie exclaimed. "Millions!"

An image of the huge Crystal Palace Hotel on the waterfront sprang into Justin's mind. It was a hotel that had probably been built with the stolen money.

As Justin finished reading the article there was a loud rap at the door. As Mr. Daniels went to answer it, Justin strained to see who the visitor was.

Justin watched as his father moved aside to allow someone to enter. It was Blackie, the author of the poison pen letters. Officer Olsen was close behind him.

"I just wanted to say how sorry I was that all of this happened," the young boy began, twisting his hands nervously. He looked apologetically at Justin, then glanced nervously at Katie and Kiel.

He was shuffling from one foot to the other as he spoke. "I knew what my stepfather's plans were for a long time, but I couldn't tell anyone. I just about told you at the cafe that day after I overheard you talking about going over to Indian Point to investigate, but I couldn't bring myself to do it," he stammered. "I hoped that the bike accident and the letters would scare you away. I'm just sorry you didn't listen to them."

He looked sadly at Kiel's hand that was still encased in bandages.

"You're not the only one," Justin said. He suddenly felt sorry for the boy, who stood uncomfortably inside the doorway with Officer Olsen standing stoically beside him. It was obvious that he had been as much a pawn in the hotel owners' game as the three young detectives.

Justin wondered fleetingly why the boy had gone to such an effort to warn them away from investigating the creature. But as he thought about it more, he realized that given the circumstances he might have done the same thing. He didn't exactly agree with Blackie's methods, but he had at least tried to steer them away from danger.

"What will you do now that your stepfather is in jail?" Katie's voice broke Justin's reverie.

"I'm going home to Saskatoon with my mother. Once I'm done answering a few question, that is," Blackie replied, then looked guiltily up at the police officer.

Officer Olsen gave him a faint smile but said nothing.

The room was uncomfortably silent before Blackie spoke again. "Well, I'd better get going." He began backing towards the door. Deep lines of unhappiness were etched on his face.

"Thanks a lot for coming over to explain," Justin said, jumping up to shake the boy's hand. "If you ever get back to Turtle Lake, make sure you stop for a visit."

"Okay," Blackie said, a smile brightening his face. "But if I do, I'll phone ahead, instead of writing a letter," he added with a nervous laugh.

Justin burst into giggles. The poison pen letters suddenly came to his mind. Soon the trailer was filled with laughter.

"Good idea!" Justin told his new friend. "Oh, by the way, I have something that belongs to you." Justin disappeared for a moment and came back holding a silver jack-knife which he handed to Blackie with a quiet wink. A moment later the three waved good-bye as Blackie followed Officer Olsen out the door.

The water was calm as the Rolands and the Daniels made their way across Turtle Lake in a large aluminum fishing boat. The children were sitting in the back of the boat, now relaxed. The mystery of the Turtle Lake Monster had been solved.

Turtle Lake was now tranquil. Most of the sightseers had gone home. More than a week had passed since the true identity of the Turtle Lake Monster had been uncovered. The disguised submarine was now in the police compound, where it would stay until after the trial.

Tonight was the last evening that Justin would be spending with Kiel and Katie. The Rolands were leaving for home tomorrow and Justin's family would be staying for the rest of the summer.

Justin knew that he was going to miss Kiel, but he would miss Katie as well. Though he sometimes found it hard to believe, they had become good friends over the course of their adventure.

As the boat sailed along, two loons cried mournfully in the distance. All was calm.

Suddenly there was a loud splashing sound behind the boat. Justin, Kiel and Katie turned to see what the ruckus was.

The water was bubbling and burbling as something large and green began to rise to the surface.

Justin looked at Kiel and Katie. There was disbelief in their eyes.

"It couldn't be," Justin sputtered.

"I don't believe it," Kiel said, shaking his head.

"No way," Katie said. "It just couldn't be."

Or could it, Justin wondered.